the Animal Game

KIRSTEEN MACLEOD

the Animal Game

TIGHTROPE BOOKS

Tightrope Books
#207-2 College Street,
Toronto Ontario, Canada M5G 1K3
tightropebooks.com
bookinfo@tightropebooks.com

EDITOR: Susan Scott
COPYEDITOR: Deanna Janovski
COVER DESIGN: Deanna Janovski
LAYOUT DESIGN: David Jang

 Canada Council   Conseil des arts
for the Arts   du Canada

 ONTARIO ARTS COUNCIL
CONSEIL DES ARTS DE L'ONTARIO
an Ontario government agency
un organisme du gouvernement de l'Ontario

Produced with the assistance of the Canada Council for the Arts and the Ontario Arts Council.

Library and Archives Canada Cataloguing in Publication

MacLeod, Kirsteen, 1961-, author
      The animal game / Kirsteen MacLeod.

Short stories.
ISBN 978-1-988040-07-3 (paperback)

      I. Title.

PS8625.L457A7 2016   C813'.6   C2016-902236-6

For Marco—
Trusted his luck, and proved it by playing

The world of dew
is the world of dew.
And yet, and yet—
Issa

CONTENTS

Island of Witches

THE MORNING OF WANDERLEI'S FUNERAL IS ONE OF THOSE perfect Florianópolis mornings. The Brazilian sky is a clean, washed blue, and the sun's warmth makes your bones sing with a deep sense of ease. Antonio, my boyfriend, manoeuvres our Volkswagen Parati—named after a resort town near Rio de Janeiro—into position. He's getting ready to hit the gas and propel us up our impossibly short, steep, curved driveway. This is always nerve wracking. If he stalls or squeals the tires, his father will come out to mock us. Too much thrust and we'll land in the path of oncoming traffic.

Today we finesse it, pausing a moment on the lip of the road to see what's coming, before turning right and descending the hill. Veering right again, we cruise the flat lake road to the mountain and zigzag up the Hill of Seven Turns—for once, free of juddering buses and trucks to stall behind on the switchbacks. Silver-white waterfalls break the dense green forest on either side of the road, permitting a glimpse of the interior.

From the top of the mountain the cemetery's entrance is visible far below, marked by a vendor's colourful hammocks, which blow like prayer flags in the wind. We coast downhill and laugh at the audacity of the black vultures that circle above the cemetery gates.

"Psychopomps," I say, "escorting the souls of the dead."

"Garbage birds, actually," Antonio replies, pointing to the dump across the street.

It's nine forty-five when we drive through the graveyard gates and pull into the parking lot. It's empty. Have we made a mistake about the time? No one is around, so we wander over to a mausoleum with a lustrous marble floor, read the names of the dead etched on stone, then stroll past a long line of open coffins on display. I find them unnerving, the sheer number and sweep of them, their readiness. I can't help but feel their invitation, and shiver at the thought of lying inside, of the pink satin maw closing down on me.

"I bought a coffin once," Antonio says as we walk back into the sunlight. His elder brother, Luis, I knew, had died tragically in an accident. Of a head injury, in his early twenties—just like Wanderlei. Antonio rarely spoke of it. I take his hand and hold it tightly.

We walk over to a wizened old man who is leaning on a shed, smoking. He's like a dry twig, brown skin shrinking in the sun. He looks Portuguese—small, with dark hair and eyes—yet lacks the sturdiness of the Azorean fishermen who populate the lake area of the island, where we live. His blue shirt is soaked with sweat, and his clothes and hands are smudged with Brazil's red earth.

"Do you know what time the funeral for Wanderlei will be?" Antonio asks.

"Ten o'clock," the old man says, puffing on his cigarette.

I blink, and then stare. Thin wisps of smoke escape from the edges of a white bandage stuck loosely over his throat. He takes another puff. Again, smoke seeps out. It's a tracheotomy hole.

"Over there," he wheezes, pointing to a group that's gathering at the foot of a nearby hill.

I'd been in Brazil for one week when Jorge, Antonio's brother-in-law, took me to see the bar in Florianópolis. On our six-hour drive up the coast, I did my best to follow his convoluted tales: something about a Nostradamus prophecy and the island sinking under the sea, and about Jorge's aunt in "Floripa" who had to be kept away from the beach—a non-swimmer, she'd dive straight into the waves, beguiled by witches. At Itaguaçu beach, he said, the most beautiful place on earth, local witches had held an extravagant party, inviting demons, werewolves, vampires, and other entities, including headless mules—which spurt fire, and are the ghosts of women cursed for fornicating with a priest in a church—and giant fire snakes called *boitatás*. But the witches had left the devil off the guest list: he stank like sulfur and had appalling manners, making everyone kiss his tail to demonstrate his power. Enraged, the devil crashed the party and turned all the witches to stone.

To this day the rocks stand in the green-blue shallows off the beach, Jorge insisted, pointing vaguely as we turned onto a long suspension bridge that led over glittering blue sea to the island. In downtown Florianópolis, capital city of Santa Caterina state, we stopped in the main square for a quick *cafezinho*, sitting on a shady bench under a spreading fig tree that was said to have magical powers. "Walk around it three times clockwise for marriage," Jorge said with a shrug when I looked unconvinced, "and seven times counterclockwise for divorce." Florianópolis, he told me, is named for Marshal Floriano Peixoto, Brazil's second president. Its historical name was Senhora do Desterro, Our Lady of Exile. Before that, it was Meiembipe, Place up the River, or Y'Jurerê-Mirim, Small Mouth, to the indigenous people. Nowadays, a reputation for the supernatural meant everyone called it Ilha das Bruxas—Island of Witches. Which, I wondered, reflects the *genius loci*, the pervading spirit of this place?

As we stood up to leave, Jorge pointed out folkloric creatures in the black-and-white stone mosaic underfoot, including a *bernúncia*, a peculiar alligator-cow cross. We hopped back into the car and sped over the green mountain to the lake. There, we crossed a small bridge where fishermen held up shrimp on hooks to passing motorists. Now that's fresh, I remember thinking. Years later I'd tell someone this story, and learn that as with so many things about Brazil, I had it all wrong: those were "advertising" shrimp, not for sale. It's hard to perceive reality in a new place.

Along the lakeside road, trees unfurled like scarves in the wind, and bright windsurfers bobbed against blue water and sky. On Rua das Rendeiras—the Street of Lacemakers—elderly women sat working in wooden shacks, white bobbins flying in dexterous hands. On the porches their fine tablecloths and garments swayed in the breeze. Then the road veered upwards again, and we pulled over on the hilltop in front of a low, boxy building with a stunning view of the lake. "This is the bar," Jorge said, pointing. He began to honk the horn at a man walking away from us down the other side of the hill.

"Who's that?" I asked.

"Our inheritance," Jorge replied with a grin. "Wanderlei will be living in the house with us."

Wanderlei ambled back up the steep incline, bare chested despite the intense November noon-hour heat. His black skin was dusted with white—sea salt. I smiled at his castaway pants, clearly used for land and sea. Strips of denim hung down in six-inch tentacles where he'd ripped the pant legs off, creating an octopus effect. His flip-flops were so worn that when he stopped in front of us, both heels rested on the searing pavement.

He looked about twenty-five, athletic, completely at ease. Unencumbered, carrying nothing, he shook hands warmly with Jorge and said "Olá," with a broad smile and a high-five for me.

"Wanderlei is the caretaker of this property," Jorge explained in our usual mixture of English, Portuguese, and charades. "In exchange for keeping an eye on things, André lets him live in the attic." André, the current owner, was in the process of selling the bar to Antonio. The plan was we'd run the place with Antonio's family and live next door. Wanderlei, I gathered, was part of the deal.

Hands liquid, Wanderlei told Jorge stories of waves. I wandered over to the bar and the small house next door, bordered by woods, where we'd soon be living. Huge pink-grey boulders marked the edge of a cliff at the front of the property, which dropped down to a tangle of banana trees, bushes, and creaking bamboo. Beyond stretched Lagoa da Conceição, the freshwater lagoon for which this part of the island was named. The intoxicating scent of an unknown flower wafted up from the cliffside and filled me with pleasure. This place was truly enchanting: gigantic rocks, opulent green foliage, hibiscus bushes with gaping pink and red blooms, profusions of yellow trumpet flowers. And in the distance, white dunes against blue sea, the green mountain, and the shining lake. So this was the spirit-haunted Island of Witches. My new home: wide open spaces, and a natural beauty so intense it seemed illusory.

Negotiations for the bar's sale made their torturous progress. André's business partner was refusing to leave, so now the matter was tied up in the courts. Meanwhile, Antonio arrived and we got to work in Lagoa, climbing the road to the hilltop to clean up. Imposing order on the house was going to take weeks. We pried off the wooden bar-band posters, erected against squatters and snoops, from the floor-to-ceiling windows. We scrubbed out the large container that sat on top of the house so the big truck from the city could fill it with water, supplementing what we would pump up the cliff face from the well. Slowly, we reclaimed the living space.

As for Wanderlei, we never saw him at the house, though we encountered him many times a day as he fished in the lake or wandered back and forth from the beaches. At home, the main reminder of his presence was a ladder out back that led up to the flat roof above our sunroom. From there he could step through a small opening and into the attic to sleep.

Wanderlei's perch was perfect for a surf devotee, equidistant from the cold, wild waters off Praia Mole, "Soft Beach," and the waves of Praia Joaquina, where international surf championships are held. With each high-five Wanderlei and I shared in passing, I admired him more. A life of freedom and simplicity was *possible*. For Brazilians, Antonio said, he was a common character, a colourful scoundrel—a *safado*. Everyone in the lake knew him and rolled their eyes when his name was mentioned. Some said he'd been living in Lagoa for five years, while others insisted it was twice that. Whatever the case, I liked Wanderlei's cool style: his mystical pentacle necklace, which he'd made out of candle wax, perfect for surfing; how he'd replied, "Pego ondas"—I catch waves, when Antonio asked his occupation.

In the evenings, Wanderlei often stopped by to share an ice-cold beer as we relaxed in a lakeside restaurant. We'd watch the fishermen pull their boats onto the sand and empty their nets, and soon after, we'd feast on fresh *tainia* fish, shrimp, a stew called *pirão*—made with manioc flour and seafood—fried potatoes, and rice. After dinner, tired and content, chairs pushed back, we'd enjoy the cool breeze off the lake that blew fresh on our faces.

One night, Wanderlei emerged from the growing shadows as our plates were being cleared.

"Hey, *cara*, I hear you made an unfortunate enemy," Jorge said, filling a glass and handing it to Wanderlei.

"This is true, *amigo*," he replied, making a curious, hunted-animal gesture.

He said no more, drained his beer, and with a wave and a concerned glance up and down the street, slipped back into the darkness. We turned to Jorge expectantly. A few days before, Wanderlei had been knocking back *cachaças* at Ferro Velho—The Junkyard—a bar down on Praia Mole, his favourite surfing beach. Night fell, and the air cooled suddenly. It started to rain. Everyone huddled under the banana-leaf roof of the *barraca* to keep dry and warm.

"Wanderlei was drunk," Jorge told us. "He was standing behind a petite, pretty woman. After a while, he just reached out and put his hand on her ass." Jorge sipped his beer, set down his glass deliberately, and looked up at us. "She was the police chief's wife."

Wanderlei had failed to register the presence of the chief, who, at five feet two, was easy to miss. Bellowing in fury and dressed in his lake police uniform—flip flops, a T-shirt and shorts, and a baseball cap—the chief had run into the rain in pursuit of the tall, muscular surfer. He didn't catch him. But now Wanderlei, sober and sorry, awaited the retribution that would surely come.

Eventually, we managed to kill off the legions of ants, the hilltop house's only inhabitants for the past two years, and move in. For now, Antonio and me, along with Jorge and his wife Jeanne, Antonio's sister—and Chico, the blue, yellow, and green family parrot, who wagged his leathery black tongue and shrieked nonstop, "Esta chuvendo, Chico, lauro, tchau"—It's raining, Chico, parrot, bye. Antonio's parents would join us closer to opening day, which we hoped would be before *Carnaval* in February.

Down at the community centre, I saw a poster that made me feel at home: a notice for a separatist slide show entitled "*Québec: un pays une culture.*" I soon met David, a freelance journalist from New York City who had married a Brazilian. For five years now, he had lived in Florianópolis on the other side of the mountain. When I told him we had just moved to Lagoa because we were buying André's bar, David frowned. Did he want to tell me something? He hesitated.

"Be careful," he said finally.

"What do you mean?"

"That place is known as a drug hangout. Cocaine."

"New management," I said with a shrug. What did that have to do with us?

Even as I brushed off the warning, I remembered André's face when he'd said, "My life was ruined here with drugs and trouble." Cocaine— maybe that explained why he was so rich. Or perhaps why his wife was divorcing him, and why he couldn't wait to get away.

"As long as the judge fixes things soon so we can open the bar, all will be well," I told David with a laugh. He didn't laugh in response. Another day, I met Roberto, the owner of the bike shop. He spoke English and had lived here for many years. We sat on the bench outside his store and chatted. I decided to ask the Brazilian what to expect here.

"Watch out," he said, "this place has an undertow."

"Of what?" I asked.

"Drugs. Depression. Damage." Waving his hand at the calm blue lake, the green mountains, he added, "This is all an illusion."

I told Antonio about these encounters. We vowed we weren't going to be put off by jaded locals. With nothing to do but wait for the court to remove André's former partner—who was somehow still in business next door at the bar—we started roaming the island's forty-six beaches. Most days, though, we lingered near the lake, often hiking the footpath in the shade of lime and orange trees to Costa da Lagoa, where we'd devour heaping plates of mussels, then, soporific, catch the boat back. Or we'd loaf at Praia Mole, five minutes' walk from the house, dozing in the sun, swimming when the waves were tame or watching the surfer fraternity paddle out into the wild waters when no one else dared.

Riding the swells, they made it look easy, like they'd tamed the sea, become one with it. Wanderlei—always in the water over his head, yet he kept his footing. Massive blue waves delivered him onto the sand.

Lazing in the hot sun under the spell of Wanderlei's physical poetry, my office cubicle seemed impossibly far away. I'd moved to this surfer island with Antonio, whom I'd been dating for nearly a year back in Toronto. There, my career as the next Oriana Fallaci had not panned out. I'd always imagined that like her, I'd travel the world as a journalist, seeking adventure and truth, maybe ripping off my chador in interviews with the Ayatollah Khomeini and throwing my microphone at Muhammad Ali for being vulgar. Instead, four years after graduation and about to turn thirty, I was working at a financial paper, adding commas to articles titled "Five Key Things to Know About No-Load Funds." Sitting in my five-by-five-foot pen, life felt unreal. Surely there was something more?

Now, home was an island 8,500 kilometres south and I was starting anew, clad in a bikini three sizes smaller than my Scottish-Canadian concept of decency allowed. Clouds billowed and blew away overhead. I had seldom felt so carefree. As Wanderlei paddled out to catch the next wave, I had a sudden awareness of the salt water flowing in my veins. Was Brazil to be my salvation? The place where I was at home in the world, and in my own skin?

The wind picked up. I wrapped my towel around my shoulders, and saw a woman on the rocky headland above the sea, black hair whipping in the blasts. She started to rock—was she laughing? Just then Antonio pointed, alarmed. A rogue wave had hit Wanderlei and dashed him under. We finally exhaled as our resident surf god tumbled out of the roiling water, gasping for air. I glanced up, and saw the woman had disappeared.

"Looks like our gatekeeper has lived to surf another day," Antonio said.

"What do you mean?"

"Wanderlei showed us the bar last year. Jorge and I were here on holidays, and we stopped in front of the 'For Sale' sign. Wanderlei came out and opened the door so we could look inside. If not for him, we'd have just driven off."

Another connection. I felt our lives and Wanderlei's were linked, though I couldn't explain how. His knowledge, about weather and waves, the habits of the dusty green lizards that climbed up from the cliffside "the size of surfboards," fascinated me. On lazy afternoons at home, we'd leave eggs on the back patio to lure the otherworldly creatures—four feet long—out from between the boulders. They'd crack open the shells with sharp teeth and claws, then lick out the insides with flicking red tongues.

Most of all, I loved Wanderlei's fantastical stories about the Island of Witches, in which malevolent spirits gathered like ill winds, stealing fishermen's boats, drinking the blood of children, and all too frequently, luring innocents to their deaths. Like most residents, Wanderlei said, he believed in black magic, in evil spirits. I immersed myself in these dark tales, some of which were written up in English, presumably for visiting tourists, and wondered at their original source. The Azoreans had a long history of island isolation before they settled here in the new world, bringing their medieval stories with them. Likely layered in were animist tales from early inhabitants such as the Tupi-Guarani, which revolve around hideous monsters. One has a snake's body with seven dog's heads that shoot fire. Another, a snake's body with a parrot's head. Add to this the mighty *orixás*, gods the slaves brought from Africa, such as Omolú, the wrathful deity of smallpox and infectious disease, with his deformed limbs and pockmarked skin. These were powerful and terrifying entities.

As I read and traced my finger along the outline of a voracious-looking witch drawn by a local folklorist, I thought about how artists give shape to unseen realities. The sorceress stood over a cauldron made from a tree root. The pot was full of severed heads. Above it she held a tiny man upside down by his leg. In her other hand was a sharp blade. I shuddered and closed the book.

Days in our sleepy island paradise continued to unfold in mellow pursuits. Sometimes we'd descend the steep cliff path beside the house, wander through the bamboo thicket and sit on the boulders beside the lake to fish. We'd take turns learning to throw Antonio's purse-seine net: hold the weights, swing your body back, then forward, release so the net opens in a wide arc, and then pull it slowly closed. More often than not, we'd make our way back up the path with a few sardines, or no fish at all, just bananas, papayas, and tangy red *pitanga* fruit picked from bushes along the way.

Despite our laid-back lifestyle, my nerves were getting jangled. One day as we set out for a swim in the calm waters of Barra da Lagoa, the car ahead of us slammed on its brakes and screeched its tires. We heard a thump. A big brown dog lay motionless on the roadside. I found it strange that no one stopped, including us. Jorge just drove on. There was no comment. We passed a few hours at Barra, then walked up to Mozambique Beach, a long, clean stretch of sand backed by cedar woods. On the drive home, I watched for the dog. The spot was marked by vultures, which lifted off in a black cloud as we approached. I thought I saw the dog's shapely head—and then its long, gleaming white spine. The flesh from the legs and pelvis was picked clean. The remains looked like a grotesque hobbyhorse.

The vultures had torn a hole through the beautiful surface of this place. This is just how it is in the subtropics, I told myself. I couldn't say why I was unnerved by what hit me like some new, deep brutality. Birds at home eat road kill. Why should it be any different here?

Another afternoon we got a flat tire and stopped at a *borracharia*, where drivers go to have their car tires patched. I enjoyed the comedy of watching seven puppies, born out back to the proprietors' dog, jumping around. One got stuck as it tried to wriggle through a hole in a wood-plank wall. It was tiny, sleek, black and brown. The owner, noticing my amusement, said, "Why not take it?"

Back at the house, the happy puppy, Maggie, quickly became a study of misery, howling and crying if she was left alone for even an instant. Antonio made her a doghouse out of an old speaker, I gave her a bone, and we stupidly tied her up in the yard, just to take a break from her lamentations. Within no time, she was gone. That day we walked along the road asking at houses, and down the paths where there were no roads, calling. We never saw nor heard a trace. One neighbour said, "She's probably dead. Something ate her." Others asked me, "What do you expect from a *vira lata*?"—a "can-turner," a stray. Just forget about it, they said.

Everyone seemed so unconcerned—about dogs, about one another. We went to say goodbye to an English couple who were closing their bar after three years, returning to Rio, bankrupt, their relationship in tatters. Again, we refused to see this as a cautionary tale. They'd had problems with drinking and drugs, but the final straw had been a robbery—orchestrated by locals, plus some other ex-pats, all of whom had worked for the couple. As the man and his distraught wife crammed their suitcases into a taxi, he said earnestly: "One piece of advice. Don't trust *anyone* here. Things are not as they seem."

By the sea, all tensions ebbed away with the tides. I'd stretch out on my towel on the sand, baking my bones, gazing out at the island off Praia Mole and imagining how it would be to swim out there. One afternoon, a lithe woman in a bikini sauntered along the shore, her dark hair blowing. Something about her was familiar. As she passed, she turned to look at me—and her face was that of a hag. I jumped, looked hard, but the sun was in my eyes. By the time a cloud passed over, all I could see was her youthful back receding down the beach. More shade, I told myself, moving shakily towards a *barraca*. I stared at the ocean to steady myself. A tune came unbidden, and then the words, about how people are strange when you're a stranger, and faces look ugly when you're alone. It's alienation, I thought with relief, brought on by unfamiliar surroundings.

My uneasiness grew. One evening, we stopped for a drink on the way home from the beach. The bar's owner, a muscular man with a martial artist's grace and a large gun stuck in the waistband of his bathing trunks, brought us a few beers. When he sat down, he told us that he actively prayed for a robber to be delivered to him.

"It would be his last final mistake," he said in English, patting the gun. I could feel my nerves on edge. Could no one else hear a dog's agonized howls coming from beyond the dune? So many strays here. I finished my drink, and ran back up the steep path to the house. I wanted to be alone, to gather my thoughts.

As soon as I sat down out back I heard a jaunty whistle. It seemed to emanate from the boulders at the edge of the cliff. Terrified, I ran inside to get a flashlight. As I cast about for intruders, the beam fell on Chico, who looked back innocently from his cage in the tree. I calmed down. It *was* him. When I moved away he began again, marching fiendishly up and down his perch, whistling in the dark.

Lately, the sound of drums at night had been filling me with foreboding, and I was having disturbing dreams. In one, the hag from the beach emerged from under the lake's surface, stretching her bony fingers up the cliff to the house. When I'd told Antonio, he confessed that he too felt unsettled. We'd been sitting up on the boulders, gazing out over the lake as the sun melted into the mountains. "So beautiful. So why doesn't all this beauty feel healing, or peaceful?" he'd asked. A sudden squawk startled me out of my thoughts. The parrot. "Esta chuvendo"—It's raining, Chico said conversationally. I shone the flashlight on him again. His beady eye had a mad gleam. Heart pounding, I rushed inside and locked the door.

In late December we headed south to Esteio, near Porto Alegre, to spend the Christmas holidays with Antonio's family. As we left, we drove down the lake road and saw Wanderlei, waist deep in the waters of Lagoa. He was fishing, walking backwards and unravelling a line and hooks wound around a pop bottle. We honked. He gave us a smile and a thumbs-up. Wanderlei's joyousness was contagious. He was unfettered. He seemed less himself than a part of everything, in flow with the currents, the wind and waves, the sky and sea. He dared to live, riding on the vast ocean. Maybe he'd teach me to surf when we returned, teach me the art of drift. I waved from the car window at his black silhouette, carved from the blue-tinged, sandy shallows.

During our two-week holiday down south, I felt out of place in Brazil's parallel universe, where each day dawned hotter and brighter than the last. I'd take refuge under the shady cinnamon tree at the end of Antonio's parents' garden. I missed my family. Even snow. Meeting my new family was slightly awkward. All they knew was that I was three years older than Antonio, divorced, Protestant, an *estrangeira*. Jeanne, and Kara, the youngest sister, lived in Esteio, as did Antonio's parents. The other four sisters had made the twenty-hour drive from São Paulo in a Volkswagen Beetle: Inez at the wheel, with Anna, Isabela, Madalena, and all their bags and presents, jammed in.

One afternoon, an elderly aunt asked me in Portuguese, "Are you Catholic?" I heard "colic" and replied that Antonio's mother had made me some curative tea and I was feeling much better. Everyone laughed, and later, the sisters called it a brilliant evasion. I was pleased; they were on my side, despite my Portuguese and other failings.

After the Christmas feast, someone played the accordion, *gaucho* music from the south of Brazil. I watched Antonio. His hair was longer and curlier than it had been in Toronto. He wore a fancy white shirt with a pair of wild-patterned cotton shorts, like he hadn't quite finished dressing. He danced with me, with his sisters, with the head and vertebrae of the Christmas fish. Later, his parents, Senhor Osvaldo and Dona Lurdes, waltzed together. Antonio took after his mother, I decided. Jorge played the guitar, and everyone sang along. The sisters talked and laughed, taught me to swear.

After New Year's, with high hopes and a million things crammed into the car, we returned to Floripa. It was a hot day, the kind that seems to make Brazilians happy. I wilt and drag myself around. At the house, as usual, there was no sign of Wanderlei other than his ladder. Unless this belongs to him, I thought, noticing a gym bag on the grass out back, with musty-looking towel and battered running shoe sticking out. Beside the bag, on the walkway that led to the back door, was a dark stain, like something sticky had been dropped on the cement.

Inez, Antonio's eldest sister, who'd stopped on her way back to São Paulo, came in talking excitedly. She had been by that morning to see whether we'd arrived home yet, and had nearly tripped over Wanderlei lying face down on the patio. At first she'd rolled her eyes and thought, *Drunk again.* But something was odd—the angle of his body, that the sun was getting hot, yet he didn't move. When she saw the blood pooling around his head, she ran next door for help. A few employees had been at the bar, cleaning up. They said they too had noticed Wanderlei lying there and had tried to wake him up—that was the night before. He'd been washing dishes for them at the bar, and drinking leftovers from the glasses. They assumed he was just sleeping it off. Inez, infuriated, insisted that they take Wanderlei to the hospital.

"So they picked him up, and threw him in the back of their truck like a sack of potatoes," she said, shaking her head.

Antonio phoned the hospital, asking if someone from Lagoa had been brought in.

"Yes, he is here," was the reply. "In fact, he just died a little while ago. Do you know the family? Otherwise he'll be buried in a pauper's grave."

Wanderlei, the wave-tamer who risked his life daily in the raging surf, had died falling off a ladder? My heart pounded. Lulled by the beauty, mesmerized, his young life stolen—by the island's malevolent spirits?

The next day, two mean-looking policemen with big guns—these were not lake cops—came to investigate the death. They climbed the ladder to look around, then stood talking beside the blood, now deep purple and baked into the concrete. We climbed up too. There was a small fire pit on the gravel-covered roof of our sunroom, with coal, a little cooking pot, and empty mussel shells. Ducking through the opening into the attic, we saw Wanderlei's worldly possessions: a blue hammock made from an old fishing net, clothes, and a straw sunhat, empty *aguardiente* bottles scattered across the floor, two halves of an old surfboard, a candle in a jar, and random pages torn from books—forty pages here, twenty pages there.

Antonio read out the names of alchemists handwritten on scraps of paper—Thomas Aquinas, Hermes Trismegistus. We descended, having found absolutely nothing to give to Wanderlei's family. The police told us their conclusion. Fractured skull. There had been no foul play—he fell from his ladder, probably drunk.

The news spread around the lake, including a rumour that the police chief had bumped Wanderlei off for touching his wife. I was struck by how little anyone seemed to care. Was it indifference, or maybe fatalistic acceptance? Or what? It was kind of like, "colourful local character does another crazy thing" with an incredulous "what next?" laugh.

Nothing next, I thought grimly.

Now, Antonio and I thank the wheezing gravedigger, exchanging a glance of horror as more smoke leaks from his bandaged throat. We walk in the direction that he's pointing. As we approach the small group standing at the foot of the hill, we notice one man is particularly distraught. The others give him sad looks. They're making gestures of sympathy.

"Wanderlei's father," Antonio says. "He adopted him about ten years ago—he and his wife."

"How could the father have an adopted son who's in his early twenties?" I whisper. The stepfather is too young, maybe thirty-five.

"Things happen here," Antonio shrugs. "Maybe he joined the stepfather's family before. Sometimes kids just show up, like stray dogs."

There are ten mourners, counting us. We are the only ones from

Lagoa. Three women in dark sunglasses hold bouquets of yellow chrysanthemums. One is Wanderlei's stepmother, and she introduces us to the others. We all fall silent when the coffin is wheeled out toward us on a gurney. Strangely, at a signal from the priest, four men, one on each corner, begin pushing the coffin straight up the hill. There is no path, just a deep gash in the sun-baked red earth where water had run downhill.

We join the odd procession. The rubber wheels of the gurney bump over the uneven ground. As the incline gets steeper, two more mourners grab the side and help to push. This increases the velocity, and the bumps become more violent. The coffin, which had seemed secure, shifts. The lid begins to move, swinging slowly open, and banging down with a little thump. No one seems to notice that Wanderlei is in danger of being catapulted out of his coffin onto the scrubby grass.

I exhale when our shortcut intersects a real path at the hilltop, and we proceed with dignity to a hole that two men have just finished digging. The coffin is lowered gently. People are speaking, but I can't understand what is being said. I look around. Wanderlei has another lovely view. Nothing could rival the vista from the house in Lagoa, but this place is full of well-tended trees and sweet-smelling flowers in bloom. I imagine that given the choice, he'd have preferred cremation so he could have been tossed into his beloved waves.

We encircle the coffin in the hole in the ground, and the priest begins to talk. The whole thing feels unreal: the comedy of the casket being pushed up the hill with the lid open; the smoking gravedigger taunting death; the irrepressible joyfulness of the cemetery itself, its pink and white tombs like icing on fanciful cakes.

This is my first funeral. I study the grief-stricken faces of Wanderlei's family, and finally, the reality of their calamity begins to register. They are white, well dressed, middle class. They had adopted Wanderlei, hoped to give him a better life. They sent him to a good school, but he'd just taken off, turning up in Lagoa, surfing and drinking. At least that's what the vegetable seller had told us when we'd asked if she knew Wanderlei's next of kin. Had he known life's ever-changing fluidity, lived in tune, as I'd believed? Or had he been running away, perhaps in pain?

I consider it, imagine Wanderlei going home in the evenings, tired after a day of riding waves, climbing up the ladder to sit on the roof, perhaps eating a papaya or a bunch of tiny monkey-paw bananas plucked from a tree along on his way. How beautiful to look out on the mountain and the lake as the red-gold sunset faded, before climbing into the attic to sleep, free as a bird in a nest. Free—or lost?

The priest's eulogy ends. The father tosses the first handful of earth onto the coffin, and begins to sob. The gravediggers stand respectfully by, hands crossed in front of them as though in church, eyes cast down, their posture incongruent with their dirty clothes, the earth and sweat stains on their sky-blue shirts. One by one we scatter our handfuls.

As I throw earth on the coffin, it all seems wrong. Wanderlei, young and vital, now dead. This man who loves him, crying. Blood stains on the pathway to our new house, our hopes. The idyllic Island of Witches, yet everyone's dreams go to hell. This place is not benign. Its beauty is a mask.

The stepfather takes a stick and begins to etch Wanderlei's nicknames in the wet cement at the head of the grave: Vandeco, Indio. Antonio's face is pinched, his thinness suddenly exaggerated. "I somehow feel responsible," he whispers. I'm sure he's reliving the day he bought a coffin, his brother's funeral. The service ends and we feel heavy with tragedy. The mourners shake hands. We say how sorry we are to the stepfather. He thanks Antonio profusely for coming, for finding him to tell of Wanderlei's death, ensuring his son was buried properly.

As we drive out of the cemetery, the gravediggers are refilling Wanderlei's tomb, undoing their morning's work. Past the gates, we speed away from the huge vultures that squat and leap, ripping with curved beaks under the duplicitous blue sky.

The Animal Game

DONA MARIA LIVES IN A SHUTTERED HOUSE IN A COMPOUND
that's locked up tight against São Paulo and its blaring car horns, its men
who urinate on the bougainvillea outside the train station, its bags of
burning rats next to the market, its hungry criminals. Her little fortress has
high walls, strong wrought iron gates, and a single, well-defended door.

Whenever someone pushes her front buzzer she shouts, "Ja vai!"—I'm
coming already!

"Quem e?"—Who is it? she demands crossly of the vague shapes
beyond the metal-fortified glass.

If it's someone she wants to talk to, which is rare, she turns the old-
fashioned key and the lock opens with a thunk. If not—or it's someone
she doesn't know, and therefore a potential home-invader—she mutters,
"Não vou abrir"—I won't open it, and shuffles away again.

We flee at the distinctive sound of Dona Maria's brown leather slippers
dragging along the patio. Within her stronghold, we've been living in a
second house for months now, since we left Florianópolis. The house
is rented by Antonio's eldest sister Inez, who is joined by fluctuating
relatives: Antonio's other sisters, and sometimes, his parents and cousins.

Dona Maria is slow, and easy to avoid—yet her presence is impossible
to escape. Most mornings, at six thirty, we are awakened by clanging pots,
putrid smells, and foul-mouthed curses as she prepares breakfast for her
only regular guests—stray cats that infiltrate her domain from the rooftops.

The old lady has moved the stove from her kitchen to the outdoor laundry area right beside our house, so now the unholy stench floats freely through our shutters. It permeates my pillow no matter how hard I press it to my face, the smell of vile sausage remnants spiced with filthy herbs—although Antonio's sisters insist that Dona Maria fattens the cats with premium chicken breast and fish, carefully deboned so the felines don't choke.

Awakened by clanging, assaulted by stink, we lie in our beds, monitoring the escalation of her temper. "Mer-da," she yells, stressing both syllables firmly. "Filhos da puta"—Sons of bitches. Then, "Sai daqui, safados"—Get out of here, you scoundrels. I drift off in the silences between her bellows.

"Estou com o saco cheio desta merda!"

Despite my despair, I can't help but smile at this one—my testicles are full of this shit. Eventually, fully outraged, Dona Maria's voice rises to a spine-chilling, sleep-banishing halt. "Nao aguento mais!" I can't stand it anymore! she screeches in a crescendo of crashing bowls hurled at the free-loading cats.

The story goes that when Dona Maria was a child, she relied on the generosity of neighbours for food. Poor but pretty, she grew up and married a much older man, a landowner. Since her husband's death many, many years ago, she's been a landlady. She is that peculiar figure in Brazil, both respected and reviled—a wealthy widow.

Viuvas ricas are esteemed for their independent means, yet are treated with contempt. Men often salivate over their money—and sexual experience, if the widows are youngish. Neighbours seem jealous and talk, knowingly, about the widow's unnatural desires. Look at her, her husband's been gone only a short time and she's already showing her knees, they might say, only sometimes speaking with irony.

After making breakfast for the cats, Dona Maria, ancient and impervious, devotes herself to business. She collects rent from us or other tenants in the villa, which is really a lane across the street with a dozen crowded-in, haphazard apartments, a sort of pigeon coop for people. And she adds to her empire by selling homemade sweets in the candy stores around the block.

At first I gorged happily on *pé de moleque*—little boy's foot, made with ground peanuts and sugar—and on cashew and coconut confections. In our large, hungry household, I did begin to wonder why the candy sat untouched except by me. Then I finally imagined Dona Maria stirring sweets, using the same spoons and the same pots as for the revolting cat food.

Somehow, even while amusing herself, Dona Maria manages to make money. She loves the *jogo do bicho*—the animal game, a street-corner lottery in which twenty-five different creatures represent numbers.

If you dream of cow shit, you must go to the corner right away and put some money on the cow, she tells me earnestly one day. A win is certain.

Founded in 1889 to raise money for Rio de Janeiro's zoo, the *jogo* has grown into a popular national pastime. Originally, zoo visitors were asked to guess at the identity of an animal hidden behind a curtain to win a prize. Despite being one of the most organized and honest institutions in Brazil, it is also illegal, run by a kind of mafia. You always get your money, people say, so no one seems to mind.

Dona Maria's devotion to the *jogo* is far stronger than any inspired by her real animals. She has a black and battered songbird that hangs in a cage in her kitchen/laundry under the constant stare of the cats. No wonder the bird sings off-key. And then there are the famished felines. Antonio's sisters find them repulsive. In the heat of the city, animals bring disease and pestilence into the carefully controlled and cleaned confines of human civilization.

"Que nojo"—How sickening, Madalena groans, holding her stomach. She refuses, no matter how stagnant the indoor air, to open her shutters to the breeze lest a filthy cat climb in and pounce on her bed.

I like cats. I don't mind reasonably clean ones on my bed. What I resent is being startled awake most days by Dona Maria's pot banging and shouting.

"Puta que te pariu"—Whore that gave you birth. "Do you think I'm your slave? Bastards. Fucking tyrants. "Vai tomando no cu"—Up your ass!

One morning, sipping my coffee on the patio, I'm startled by Dona

Maria's lusty bellows. She begins kicking the cats, pushing them off all surfaces, throwing pots and spoons. With the forbearance of the forlorn, the cats skulk off and keep their distance, blinking at her expectantly. She glares back and, in a voice of cold fury, says: "Vou matar todas"— I'll kill you all.

One week later, it's a suffocating, stiflingly hot São Paulo day. Pollution from the cars of twenty million-plus inhabitants and hundreds of belching factories is sealed into the mountain-ringed bowl of the metropolis. It's no surprise tempers are frayed.

As usual, Dona Maria is brawling with the cats. I whine to Antonio about being tired of living with so many people. Madalena snaps at Dona Lurdes, my soon-to-be mother-in-law, for not putting enough salt in the beans. Finally, after lunch, the morning's tension fades into torpor—some of the sisters return to work, other members of the household retire for a nap, and Antonio and I loll at the table, leaning on our elbows. We smile as we hear Dona Maria approach; she drags her slippers as if slowly sanding the patio. As she passes our half-closed kitchen door, she starts to speak, each sentence punctuated by a long, calculated pause.

"Oh, that poor cat is so sick."

"Someone needs to take pity and kill it."

"I wish my dear husband were here."

She lets this hang in the air a few long moments, then adds: "I think I'd better ask Antonio if he can help me take care of it—maybe even *all* of them."

Antonio and I exchange looks of alarm, wait in silence until we hear the lock thunk behind her. Then we creep outside and over to her outdoor kitchen. The feline population, usually steady at around six, has doubled. They are draped lazily on the chairs, the counters, the cool terracotta stones of the patio, even the tabletop.

In a box in one corner we spot a scruffy, nicotine-coloured cat. Its eyes and nose are crusted shut with dried mucus, which makes its fur stick up in tufts. The cat is barely breathing. It looks like a dead creature left in the hot sun to mummify.

My stomach tilts. "I thought she took care of the cats," I wonder aloud.

"She feeds them," Antonio replies. "*Meu santo*. This must be the one she wants me to kill."

"Come on," I say, leading him resolutely back to the house. We push the festering, skinny cat from our minds and decide to explore the city. We walk to the corner to catch the anarchic express to the Centro. In true entrepreneurial Brazilian style, somebody simply shows up with a bus, which we know is an illegal one because it's dirtier, more dented, and faster than a city bus—provided, of course, we don't crash. Vagabond as our lives right now.

The bus arrives. We climb aboard and hang on. The windows rattle alarmingly as we fly downtown and the driver keeps crossing himself. Years later, someone tells me that Brazilian motorists do this whenever they pass a church—and not, as I'd believed, because they believe death in traffic is imminent.

Defiled urban vistas blur past, illuminated by flashes of flowering *ipê* trees, with their vivid yellow or purple blossoms. We descend shakily at Praça da Sé, near the city's traditional heart, where the Jesuits founded São Paulo in 1554. They built their chapel in what was then a green, sweeping mountain valley, seventy kilometres from the sea.

We walk toward the fountains and forbidding neo-Gothic cathedral in the centre of the square. As we get nearer we see the street kids, little sparrows without the solace of trees, their backs against the church walls. Faces pressed into plastic bags, they sniff glue, kill hunger, transform themselves into fearless birds of prey that swoop mercilessly down on passersby, stealing their valuables.

I keep an eye out, especially after a photo I saw in *Folha de São Paulo*. It showed a kid in midair, about to land with both feet on a man's back to knock him down the church steps. It's hard to believe, such small children. I look into the faces of the nearby merchants. I've read other news reports detailing how shopkeepers, tired of little criminals, pay off-duty police to exterminate them. In Rio, eight children were murdered when gunmen, some of them cops, shot into a group of seventy street kids as they slept beside the Church of Our Lady of Candelária.

Around the dirty *praça*, genuine snake-oil salesmen make pitches into battery-pack microphones. Their patter never falters, about herbs and potions—some displayed in jars with huge, dead snakes curled inside—that will relieve all sickness and misery. People stop to listen to these evangelizing pharmacists, survey the barks and seeds and powders in open cloth bags arranged on tarps. *Old native secrets, step up for this miracle potion from the Amazon,* one vendor shouts, passing out shots of lurid blue liquid in plastic cups.

That evening, when we arrive back at the house, shadows are stealing mercifully onto the patio while a pinky-orange sun sinks into the haze. I drop into a chair with a reviving *caipirinha*—sugar-cane alcohol, crushed lime, sugar, and lots of ice—and think of São Paulo's unplanned cityscape, what it reflects about the place and about my own inner landscape: uncertainty, chaos, pleasing anarchy. Antonio, as usual so active that he seems as though he's had one too many *cafezinhos*, is banging around in the laundry/cooking area. Every now and then I glance up and see him working. He's toying with the smog-stunted plants, hanging something on the clothesline, filling a garbage can with water, playing with a piece of rope.

It's a while before I notice the silence. I lean over in my chair and see Antonio standing stock-still, staring intently. Behind his back he holds a heavy cast-iron frying pan. Slowly, he raises it high over his head, and then sweeps it down as if he were clobbering an intruder in an old slapstick movie. Moments pass. He walks forward a couple of paces, lifts the frying pan again, mutters something, and swings it down hard. I hear the pan clatter noisily across the stovetop. He stalks off and then, over the sounds of water running and clothes being scrubbed—the washing machine is broken again—I hear his fluent, fervent curses.

The clank of the key turning the lock signals Dona Maria's return. She enters, shuffles slowly by. "All those cats," she says. "What is a poor old lady to do?" Her eyes look unusually clear and shrewd. "I'd ask Antonio," she says, "but I know he doesn't have the courage. Not like his father. If only Osvaldo were here," she laments, heaving a mighty sigh.

I pretend not to understand. "I'm feeling much better thanks," I reply.

Dona Maria rolls her eyes slightly with that foreigners-are-so-dense look and continues on. Sadly for him, Antonio has no such feint. Yet she moves right past without comment—which I take to mean he's crouched down out of sight, behind the supply cabinet. Once she goes inside, I tiptoe over. He's filling a tall plastic bucket with water, and, with earnest concentration, trying the garbage can lid and assorted scraps of plywood to see which will fit on top most tightly.

"You are going to drown it?" I say, incredulous.

"Well, either that," he replies, trying another potential lid, "or I was trying to think of a way to hang it."

At nightfall, the sisters return from work one by one, rinse off the day in cleansing showers, and we all gather around the big kitchen table. The city sinks into a profound quiet as the streets transition to night's citizens, the druggies, dealers, and thieves. I begin to imagine everyone else—in condos and mansions surrounded by walls topped with broken glass and barbed wire, protected by guards; in small houses like ours, secured with steel and iron and shutters; in permeable shacks in *favelas* perched on hillsides or huddled under bridges—all going inside. In place of the city's hum and the roar and squeal of buses, soft singing from the church down the block carries on the evening air.

Dona Lurdes smooths the red-checked cloth, turns on the propane from a tank beside the stove, strikes a match, and lights the burner under the kettle and milk pot. We watch her as she moves about the kitchen, pouring water over the fragrant coffee grounds, putting it into a thermos, laying out fresh white rolls, cheese, and jam for supper. It's taken a while, but I enjoy this meal now. I'm past thinking the family is trying to torment me by eating breakfast at nine in the evening, complete with high-octane caffeine.

"Dona Maria wants me to kill one of her cats," Antonio says to Inez with a look of appeal.

"I wish you'd kill all of them," she replies. "She gave them poison once and then watched them all stagger around until they died."

"You mean this happens all the time?" Antonio asks.

"Yeah," Inez replies. "She feeds them, gets sick of them, and then they have to be killed."

"All of them?" I ask. "But why does she do it? Why does she feed them?"

There's a long silence. Dona Lurdes sits down, pours coffee from the thermos into her cup, fills it with hot milk, and stirs in two heaping spoons of sugar. Her thin face is thoughtful.

"Things are complicated in Brazil," Dona Lurdes says softly.

The next day, Antonio's father arrives from the south. By nightfall, twelve cats have been killed with a farmer's efficiency, their bodies disposed of in the garbage. For a blissful interlude, our mornings are quiet. We sleep long and well, until the abandoned cats creep back over the rooftops to feed at Dona Maria's kitchen.

Residents

"MY MOTHER WANTS TO DIE." PETER SAYS THIS MATTER-OF-FACTLY, like when he tells you his bike is broken, or that his little brother is the smart one.

I look at him closely. His hair is jet black, he's missing a few front teeth, and his skin is pale, unmarred. "Are you sure?" I ask. "Why would she want to die?"

"Because she hates herself," he shrugs.

He hands me his flattened soccer ball and follows me to the shed. He holds the ball steady as I put the pin in, attach the bike pump, and secure the base with my feet.

"Ready?" I ask, still wondering, *Can a six-year-old really know something like that?*

"Ready," he replies, fidgeting, poking at shards of broken glass on the floor with the toe of his plastic flip flop. I pump, push my thumb on the ball to feel whether it's full, and hand it to him.

"Enough air?"

"Yup. Thanks."

I watch him run, free and headlong, down the driveway. I pull the shed door shut, securing the top with a wire we rigged up to keep out the pesky neighbourhood kids.

Back inside, I pull out the cutting board and collard greens and start making dinner. It's been my new routine since I've been home recovering:

purposeful activity for an aimless body. I hear the ball bouncing outside, its sound punctuated by wild laughter as the kids play in the driveway next door. Soon, there's silence, then the doorbell rings. There's a cloth in the mechanism to muffle the bell, so now it just makes a strangled sound. I smile and don't bother to answer. I know who's there.

A moment later, children's feet slap along the driveway and past my kitchen window. Little Allie yells, "Pizza-man!" and laughs at his same old joke. Then they're all on the back porch, pushing each other out of the way to squint in through the screen door.

"Hell-low," yells Peter.

"Hell-low," echoes his brother Larry, who is four.

"Hello," I shout back. "What are you guys doing?"

They all laugh and jostle for position, dancing around. They crave the attention of adults, and these days, I'm far too easy to find. Peter and Larry live right next door, sharing the wall of our semi-detached house in Little Italy; Allie and his sister Susan live in the next semi one door down.

"We came to tell you something very important," Peter says.

They stop pushing, stand straighter, and look as serious as a little band of rogues can look.

"Jonathan is missing."

They all nod gravely.

"But I just saw him half an hour ago, playing out front. Are you sure?"

"Yes, and his family are all looking for him," Susan says excitedly.

I walk outside and see Peter and Larry's mother on her back porch. She's wearing a long-sleeved T-shirt, even though the day is hot. I wave and call, "The kids say Jonathan is lost."

She looks serious, answers in Cantonese. I realize I don't know her name.

"I hope they find him soon," I call after her as she slips back inside. "You kids let me know as soon as he turns up, okay?"

They scatter, and I step back into the kitchen. Somehow I'm not worried about Jonathan. My thoughts keep returning to what Peter said about his mother.

She's younger than she first appears. Her skin is smooth, but her posture is poor. She's bent, as though she's suffered some great, aging calamity. Bony-thin, she rarely leaves the house except to take the kids to school, when she limps along, one leg dragging. She seems devoid of energy, yet it's always her we hear through our shared wall, voice shrill, spurting an endless torrent of words. We can't tell whether she is angry or if this is just the way she talks.

The day the "zoo poo" arrived is the only time I've seen her look happy. Actually, it was compost, but neighbourhood rumour held that the city had dropped a hill of elephant shit at the end of our street for residents to use in the gardens. Peter had yelled at us, incredulous, "It's free!" He, Larry, and their mother, her face aglow, then ran home, staggering under the weight of buckets overflowing with manure.

I turn and pour olive oil into the pan, flick on the gas, and wait a moment before pushing in the thin-cut collards. I wonder why we never hear Peter and Larry's father. We see him in the garden, working on his bok choy and tomatoes, or going back and forth from the shed, where he keeps his pigeons. Peter says he raises the birds to eat. The father says no—"Hobby."

I don't believe him. He's a practical, frugal man. He has no grass or flowers; everything is dug up for a garden. The whole family wears the most basic of clothes, always clean, with their second set drying on the clothesline.

I remember one day Peter knocked on our door, agitated. "You left your porch light on—*all day!*" he said.

Another time we gave Peter a little flowerpot, so he could grow something in it. He couldn't believe our largesse. Then he asked, "How much does this cost?"

The father's hair is grey. There is a rumour. That these are not the parents, they are the children's grandparents. He's always in a hurry, and the kids never run up to him when he comes home from work. Near him they are quiet, reserved, what looks like well behaved.

He talks to us, but his English is so bad it's difficult to catch more than the general subject. On the exceptional occasions his opinions come through clearly, they're definite, even strident. He insists, for example, that eating too many vegetables makes you stupid.

I smile at the thought, turn off the collards, and walk outside to gather greens for a salad. I bend slowly, careful of the tiny incisions on my belly.

Discomfort today, not pain, so my thoughts flow on. Vegetables make you stupid. The neighbour reminds me of a guy I knew back in Brazil, on the island. He was convinced that bread goes mouldy if you put it in the freezer. Nothing anyone could say persuaded him that food gone green and fuzzy might have something do with the frequent power outages.

I knock slugs off the leaves I'm picking, shaking my head. Home is just as strange and exotic as any distant land. Perhaps this crazy theory about veggies has some basis in Chinese medicine, something he can't explain in English. Or maybe it's just a whole different view. He once loaned me a kung fu magazine. Inside was a pinup of a female action star. She was quoted as saying that in China, she has to hide her arms because they are muscular. "People say, 'That's not natural.' But in LA, people say, 'Great arms.'"

I wonder what the Chinese think about people without children. As I pick snow peas, Peter's inquisitive face appears on the other side of the chain link fence.

"Jonathan's found ..." he says.

"That's a relief. Where was he?"

"... and the police are charging the family seventy-five dollars an hour *for two hours* because the grandmother forgot he went to Canadian Tire with his dad!"

I laugh, and Peter smiles a pleased, good-boy smile. Sometimes he's so soft, and other times so cutting.

"That kid is going to be a critic," complained a friend of mine one evening. We had been sitting on the front porch drinking wine, when Peter walked up and glared at him.

"Are you an idiot? You are *smoking*," Peter had shouted. Then gently, with curiosity, "Do you want to die?"

I stand up from picking snow peas just as Peter and Larry round the corner into the garden—for the tenth time today. Kids get bored in the summertime. But Allie and Susan go swimming every day, and have their grandparents and lots of aunts and cousins to amuse them.

"Why don't you ever go to the pool?" I ask the boys, adding a silent, *instead of bugging me*. Though lately, their presence gives me strange comfort.

Peter shrugs. "I don't know where the pool is."

I feel guilt as I shoo them away. Peter looks sad but goes. Larry clings to my hand, then runs after his brother. How odd for them: Chinese parents who barely speak English, though they have lived here for ten years, and these two are both little Canadians. Larry has been saying "frucking assholes" right in front of the parents all summer long.

By the time I've finished preparing the salmon, Antonio has come home.

"So, I hear you had tea and gingersnaps earlier," he says in greeting.

There's no need to ask me about my day; the kids tell him everything before he gets through the front door.

"How are you feeling?"

My eyes well up. "I'm okay."

"Does it hurt?"

"No. It's more getting used to the idea."

"I know," he says, and pulls me close.

"So you don't think we are cursed by God?" We'd read that in many cultures, a childless person is considered dead, lacking a link to the next generation to grant them posterity.

"Not cursed," he says, kissing my head. "I prefer the other view."

I brighten, hoping for something more palatable.

"You're a sorceress who kills living things—you know, causes milk to curdle as it stands, whose glance makes cows lose their calves, who strokes the throats of children until they die..."

We both burst out laughing. Margaret Mead writes that throughout history, childless women have induced fear, been accused of being witches.

"Well, just last week, Tokyo's mayor told the *Financial Times* that it's 'futile as well as criminal' for women to continue living after they have lost their reproductive ability," I inform Antonio as we fill our plates.

He rolls his eyes, whispers, "Yes, criminal." He leans in for a long kiss. Then he opens up the door with a flourish. We go outside, to the table under our back window. Within seconds, Peter is at his back window looking down at us.

"What are you doing?" he calls.

"Eating dinner," Antonio replies. "What are you doing?"

"Nothing."

"Why don't you sing something for me?" Antonio asks. *Sotto voce*, he says to me, "I have to divert his attention somehow. I can't play chess with him anymore. He's getting too good."

We laugh, and Peter presses his face up against the screen of the back window. He sings "O Canada," twice through, before we hear his mother's voice, and he disappears.

It's dusk, shadows are forming, and the neighbourhood is suddenly quiet. It's the hour when little kids are getting soapy in their baths, preparing for bed, and backyards revert to adult territory.

We go in. I hear Antonio talking on the phone upstairs while I make some tea. I return to the yard, walk over the grass. It's cool on my bare feet. I sit at our concrete table, which looks like a sacrificial altar dropped on the lawn—courtesy of our Italian landlords. I often come home to find Antonio sitting here cross-legged, juggling or playing the guitar, with the neighbourhood kids lounging at his feet, clapping.

Tonight, I pull up a plastic lawn chair to savour the quiet. The Portuguese neighbours who call us the "single couple" are away camping. Allie and Susan and their extended Filipino family won't be home until late, as they are celebrating a hundred years of independence from Spain. The only light comes from next door. It bathes a white wall, bare except for a Chinese calendar.

I exhale into a moment of perfect peace.

"Hell-low," says a voice.

I don't answer, in hope that he'll give up.

A pause, then, "What are you doing?"

"I'm drinking some tea."

"I'm holding a flower in the window. Please look. Do you see it?"

I turn. "No, Peter, I can't see it because of the screen."

Another pause, and then, "Okay, look now, at this."

A spray of water shoots out the window, hits a passing moth. "Do you see the sparkles?"

"Yes, Peter, I see the sparkles. They're magical."

"I have to go to bed now."

"Okay, sweet dreams."

The light goes out, and I'm left alone in the warm darkness.

How peculiar it is that we all live in this same space, in our brick boxes, a wall's breadth from one another, yet our lives barely touch. Except for the kids, little envoys between adult countries.

"My mother wants to die," I remember Peter saying.

She who possesses what we most desire, and will never have.

I hold these thoughts as stars fade randomly in and out of sight. The full moon slowly discharges from the treetops, a gold seed drifting in the dark night sky. Reggae music plays down the block, the sound carries on the breeze. I hear it, sometimes loud and full, other times quiet and keening, like a heartbeat.

Horticulture

IT'S MONDAY MORNING. I PUSH OPEN THE FRONT DOOR OF THE flower shop, and the chimes jangle Rusty awake. He stands up to bark at me in fat outrage.

Rusty is a sausage dog—a *daschund*, his owner insists we call him. Today his little basket is lined with a gold silk scarf. A pink lily, the fragrant one that's popular for graduations, is woven into the wicker.

Meu santo. In Brazil, we have guard dogs, not these North American lap dogs. As I reach over to stroke Rusty's glossy head and pacify his barking, Ben emerges from the back room.

"Russell, shut up!" he yells, pointing an accusing finger at the dog. "I thought you were deaf."

"Rusty has selective hearing," I tell Ben. "Like an old person." I instantly regret this last phrase.

"How dare you say that Russell is old?" Ben pronounces "old" with disgust. He gives me the disdainful look he usually reserves for people wearing unfashionable shoes.

His face looms closer to mine. I search it for humour. He is one of those unstoppable black trains, puffing and gathering steam. "Russell is in his prime," he continues, stomping his foot and spilling coffee onto his pant leg.

I remind myself to adopt a more guarded look. People often know what I'm thinking by looking at my face, like there's a teleprompter running across my forehead.

My wife and some other Torontonians had been trying to convince me that people and their dogs often look alike. Until now, I thought they were just having a little sport with a foreigner. But as Ben continues to rant, I see that he and Rusty do share a certain Godiva-chocolate-and-bun-fed look. Ben's hair, newly dyed, is a false echo of Rusty's copper sheen.

The volume of Ben's tirade spikes and interrupts my thoughts. "You have a lot of nerve, Antonio. From now on, I want you to keep your comments to yourself, do you hear? I won't tolerate this, this insubordination."

I nod, not allowing even the tiniest hint of laughter to creep into my face.

"Get to work, we've got lots to do today," he snaps, looking cheated.

That's what you get for hiring a pacifist, I smile to myself. I walk to the back room to set down my knapsack. Sighing, I pick up handfuls of twigs from the floor. Ben always tosses the ends over his shoulders as he works.

"I think that went really well." Bartholomew, my other boss, specializes in irony.

I begin helping Bart with the roses, removing the thorns with a knife. It strikes me how much he looks like the men on Sunday night's TV show, *Brideshead Revisited*. They all wear tweed, go shooting with male friends, then sit in leather-bound smoking rooms with cigars and cognac. I can't figure out how Bart turned out to be a gay florist.

Before I came to Toronto a year ago this month, I'd never met a gay man who admitted it. Where I come from, they would be beaten. In the south of Brazil men are cowboys, riders on the *pampas* who rope steers, eat steaks over open fires, and fight for amusement. I guess I never did fit in. Not there, or here either.

Bart and I exchange tiny smiles. He is laying the delicate roses on green ferns, humming his beloved Bach to himself. Suddenly, the musical equivalent of a jab in the ribs blares through the speakers: "Do you believe in life after love..." Bart convulses, drops a rose from nerveless fingers to the floor.

He shoots me a worried glance. Both of us sense a major mood disturbance is moving in. "Let's check his coffee level," he says.

We hover behind Ben. "Still has half a cup to go," I whisper. We exchange concerned looks, like siblings whose drunken father is going to get unpredictable after that next glass.

I glance at the clock. Two minutes to nine. "We better pull up our boots," I say. Ben gives me a pitying look.

"Yes, otherwise we'll be caught left-handed," he replies. I realize I've mixed up the words once again.

For some reason, Ben isn't nearly as mean to me as he is to everyone else. I'm actually fond of him. I find something appealing about his brutal honesty—or stunning rudeness, depending on your perspective.

Last week, a client came in and asked for a ten-dollar bouquet.

"Sorry, I don't know how to do cheap arrangements," Ben told him.

I have to admit I enjoy it whenever I hear customers ask for bows on their flowers.

"No. We only have things that are in good taste here," Ben responds.

Considering the mood he's in today, I'm glad it is Monday, delivery day. *Graças a deus*, deliveries are my job. I'll be out of the shop carrying baskets to nearby offices and apartments. With luck, I'll bypass Ben's temper and avoid the two jobs I dislike: dealing with customers and making the flower arrangements.

Avoiding the customers is easier for me. My English is convincingly unintelligible when I want it to be. Also, Ben and Bart explained to me that Forest Hill matrons depend on gay men to be their arbiters of good taste—as a mere straight man, I'm not really equipped. I wonder if I'll ever be able to comprehend this society.

For the flower arrangements, unfortunately, I do somehow have the needed sophistication. I love plants—orange trees, *bananeiras*, and the endless green profusion are what I miss more than anything about home. But I detest arranging. It's ridiculous to detract from the natural beauty of the flowers by putting them in stupid baskets with sticks and fake birds and ornaments. I prefer a spare style: say, a simple glass base with little spikes upon which to set a couple of stems.

Since the day Ben told me off for the sin of mixing yellow with pink, I realized that making arrangements is more trouble than it's worth for ten dollars an hour. I prefer to clean buckets. Or mop the floor, singing the words of my latest North American discovery, the magnificent Tom Waits. "Tom do this, Tom do that, Tom … don't do that."

Or grate thorns from roses as I ponder the ludicrous expense and effort of flying them all the way from Holland and Ecuador so they can wilt in company reception areas and the windows of socialites in this godforsaken northern city. *Ca-nada*, my Brazilian relatives joke. In Portuguese the country's name means, "Here—is nothing."

Many South Americans think of the North as an inverted hell, with snowstorms instead of fires. Last winter, my first, I learned the hard way that I must not express my real feelings. People get insulted, think I have a superiority complex, ask why I don't just go home. Itchy skin, bulky clothes, indoor malls that go on for miles, darkness, dead trees: it feels like prison for someone used to warmth and sunlight.

I really want to like it here. The truth is I find Toronto sad, so pathetically endowed when it comes to sunshine, so hopeless in climate that nothing grows half the year. There's a greenhouse full of plants downtown called Allan Gardens. My wife dragged me there in midwinter to smell a *pitanga*, thinking it would make me feel better. But it was just depressing, on par with trying to celebrate *Carnaval* at a stuffy downtown hotel in February.

We've decided to try living here because she doesn't want to live in Brazil anymore. Too hot, she says, and too violent—its own kind of prison. It truly is a wonderful freedom to be able to walk the streets safely at night. *Graças a deus*, there are a few things I do appreciate. I decide to bring home a bouquet of pink and yellow roses tonight, and the orange lilies she likes.

I pull today's delivery list down off the bulletin board and scan it, noting the usual: Rolex, Loblaws, the Catholics, Imperial Oil, lots of residentials. I begin to check off the arrangements that are ready to go.

"Want to hear the 'non-complaints' from Saturday?" Ben asks, brightening. Conflict always cheers him up.

"Remember the people who ordered two bouquets for their two daughters? And they asked for two different arrangements? They phoned today to say that both girls liked the same one, and asked what they should do." He opens his eyes wide and gives us a long look over the top of his glasses, pausing for effect.

I grin slowly, despite myself. "So what did you tell them?"

"I said," and he sticks a hand on his hip, "I am a florist, not a family therapist, and you will just have to work it out for yourselves."

I look at Bart. He nods. "Yes, he did say it in exactly that tone of voice. Another repeat customer."

"I have to be myself," Ben shrugs. "And what you see, this is me actually *trying* to be nice."

I keep reading the addresses on my delivery list, imagining Ben if he didn't really try: a rampant little id with handfuls of pointed sticks, puncturing things as it runs.

"Then there was the one who didn't believe we'd delivered the flowers because he hadn't received a thank-you card yet."

"Another poor loser," Bart laughs.

It always makes me melancholy: aimless people with so little of importance going on in their lives, sending flowers back and forth just hoping to get some human contact.

When I say things like that out loud, everyone tells me to save my sympathy for people who need it—and this does not include our wildly wealthy clients.

Everyone except Ben avoids saying this when Mary, one of our co-workers, is around. They call her a rich, bored Rosedale housewife, say she works part-time in the shop "just for fun."

Mary is sweet, and she's informed me about what she calls the "language of flowers" and their important role in her social milieu: essential for entertaining, part of the whole package when setting a table or adding drama to the salon, or for conveying messages prettily, with style.

While the heedlessness of these society women about money horrifies me, I'm kind of impressed. It's like watching someone commit a sin with no guilt at all. I can't help admiring that. When Mary orders flowers, I've noticed that the more expensive the orchids, the happier she is. As for me, I carry the headless plants home on my bike, saving them from the compost heap, giving them a retirement home among the violets and hibiscuses on my windowsills.

The door-chimes jolt me out of my thoughts and awaken Rusty. Ben is too busy to yell about his barking. Mary has arrived. That means it's nine thirty already—we need to hurry.

"Hello darlings. How are my little blossoms today?" Mary calls out.

Ben hurries over and kisses her on both cheeks. "Flawless as ever, darling," he replies. "Would you like some?" Ben never shares his coffee with anyone except for Mary—and Rusty.

"*Bwen-ass di-ass*," Mary coos to me as she passes. I've been teaching her a little Spanish so she can talk to her Chilean maid. Like most North Americans, she assumes that since I'm from Brazil, Spanish is my first language. I don't bother to mention that I learned it in Toronto while waiting tables at Segovia, my first job.

One afternoon, while we were working alone, Mary had confided to me that she'd been having problems with the maid.

"What's happening?" I asked, ready to provide whatever Spanish phrases would be most helpful.

"Well, she lost my black brassiere..." Mary replied, holding up the fingers on her left hand, ready to enumerate issues.

"Wait a minute. Your husband is Chilean. Why can't he talk to her?" I asked.

She looked distressed, replied in a low voice, "He said he wasn't going to waste his time on anything to do with the help, that it's my job."

So I taught her *Donde esta*—Where is...; *No pierdas mi sujetador negro*—Don't lose my black bra; and *Esto no esta limpio*—This isn't clean. We decided that was enough for one day when she got confused trying to say, "Always put the pink paper in the pink bathroom and the blue paper in the blue bathroom."

Right now, my difficulty is to get out of the store by ten o'clock to make my deliveries without triggering Ben. If I don't get going on time, everything will be late. When I'm behind schedule, his lectures are usually the reason. Explaining this to him is unacceptable defiance. Logic doesn't enter into it.

I notice an unfamiliar name on my list. "Who is Peggy Branksome?" Both Ben and Bart stop what they are doing, and turn, eyes widening in that "Oh my dear—you don't know?" kind of way.

"Instructions for the Peggy delivery," Ben says. "One: Put the plant down in front of the door. Two: Knock, really loud. Three: Run as fast as you can for the elevator. Four: Do not, I repeat, do not look back!"

Bart nods. "Remember, under no circumstances are you to deliver it in person. We made this mistake, and look what happened to us." His face is grave.

I look back and forth for an explanation. Finally Ben exclaims, "That's what made us gay!"

"She lives all alone, is about ninety, and answers the door with nothing on, or with a tea towel pressed to her chest," Bart is looking queasy. "It's like, 'Oh, my, I'm nude again,' and she's kind of apologetic, like she forgot your name or something. By the way, she phoned today to ask if someone could take her library books back. I told her we were too busy this week and she'd have to find someone else."

"I could do that for her," I say, imagining the poor old lady, all alone and helpless.

"I'm Antonio and I want to save the world," Ben mocks.

"Listen, forget all you've heard about the gay gene. If you love your wife, heed our warning," Bart says.

"It's nine forty-five—we'd better hurry," I reply. I pick up some carnations to put into an inexpensive arrangement and think about how I really *like* yellow and pink together.

Ben, probably still puzzling over why I would want to help old ladies with their library books, says, "You know, sometimes when I'm nice, I feel embarrassed."

I'm grateful to Peggy. She's diverted Ben's attention. At ten on the dot, I pick up the first box and head out the door.

The day is cool, and the chilled breath of autumn propels my steps faster. First stop, Rolex. A young woman with "Deborah" on her name-tag, is rude to me. Her expression tells me she has piles from sitting in the reception all day.

Time passes quickly: up and down stairs and elevators, in and out of receptions, back and forth to the shop in a fast-forward flurry of motion. Rusty pops up like a Jack-in-the-box each time I enter. Then he barks and Ben yells. On and on it goes. By four thirty, only Peggy's box remains.

"Don't forget our words," comes the chorus. Ben and Bart stop to look at me as though they might never see me again.

"You can count on me," I say. I elbow my way out the door and onto the street.

"Don't tilt the arrangements," Ben roars at my back.

Last delivery of the day. My arms and legs ache. I push the button for the eleventh floor, and when I get off, I rest a moment, box balanced on the railing, looking out the window at the ravine, tinged with autumn's glorious reds and yellows. It snakes southeast and down to the blue lake beyond. I inhale the restorative colour, draw in the raspberry scent of red roses, and feel refreshed.

I consider knocking on the door and waiting, curious, part of me still wanting to help the old lady with her books. I decide I might regret it. I set the flower arrangement down gently, rap on the door, and race around the corner to the elevator.

Back outside, I sprint across the road in front of a red streetcar that's pulling into the subway station, and stand in front of the shop. Juniper Group is traced on the sign. The window is full of greenery, punctuated by expensive orchids and exotica, even birds of paradise like the ones that grow wild along the creek at the *fazenda* back home. I've finished my work with ten minutes to spare.

When I enter, there is a strange hush. I look up to see Rusty, Ben, and Bart looking at me with interest.

"So?" Bart says, "Do you feel any different?"

"I don't think so. Why?"

"Are you gay now?" Ben demands.

"Oh—Peggy. No. I followed your advice, every detail."

Bart says, "Oh." He is silent a moment, then adds, "I guess it could be true that you really are straight."

"Maybe he is," Ben says. "Yesterday I was saying how Charles was a worthless human being, that you can tell by the cut of his jacket. And Antonio said to me, 'Come on, Ben, you can't judge someone by how they dress.'"

Bart and Ben exchange disbelieving looks.

I start rinsing out buckets and try to change the subject by asking Ben about his recent holiday by the sea.

"If I had two weeks to live I'd go back there," he replies.

"So you liked it?" I prompt.

"No, because it felt like time took an eternity to pass there."

We all laugh, and then Bart asks Mary whether she enjoyed the opera over the weekend. "How was *Parsifal*?"

"I fell asleep," she says, laughing ruefully. Hockey is more her thing.

"Horticulture," Ben says.

Bart frowns at him.

"What did you say, Ben?" Mary asks.

"Horticulture," he repeats. "As in, you can lead a whore to culture, but you can't make her like it."

Mary bursts into tears. Bart puts an arm around her shoulder and glares at Ben, who looks pleased with himself. Since Mary asked for a raise last week he's been ruthlessly mean to her.

I slip off to the back room. Maybe now things will be calmer. Last week was insane—Rosh Hashanah. Everyone needed flowers before the sun went down.

I prop open the back door with a red milk crate and sit in a shaft of sunlight to enjoy a quiet smoke. Big wispy clouds wash by in the blue sky-stream, ephemeral as my thoughts, which also pass like clouds.

I draw again on my cigarette, inhale a comforting sense of accomplishment. Then I exhale a big waft, and watch the smoke dissipate into the air. I can relate to Mary in a way.

A new cloud, a white rose, is passing overhead when it hits me. Everything here dies once a year. Unlike the endless bougainvillea of the tropics, this flora is cleanly killed, and regenerates from nothing. All that takes root here, completely new and vital.

Faith Healer

"I'M GOING TO SEE DR. FRITZ," DONA LURDES SAYS. INEZ STOPS
pouring the coffee and glares at her mother.

"If you want to consult a charlatan, that's your business." Inez picks
up a spoon and gouges the sugar. "But I'm not taking you—leave me
out of it."

Dona Lurdes doesn't argue, though she knows that Dr. Fritz is seeing
patients on the other side of the city—which in São Paulo is very far.
She is a woman of quiet faith.

After breakfast, she spreads her X-rays on the table, points out her
esophagus, her cancer. Though she never says "cancer," only that she
has "an ulcer." Antonio and I are visiting from Toronto because Dona
Lurdes, his mother, is dying. She is unable to sleep, has pain in her
kidneys. She tries to eat special food to keep her strength up. Always
thin, she's now spectral. As she leans forward to explain it all, I see the
red lines on her bony chest, which circle and sweep like rivers drawn on
her skin. Targets for radiation, tracing the tumours.

At noon, Dona Lurdes and I go to the street market, where she holds
up tropical fruit for my camera. Amid the voluptuous mangoes and leafy
greens she looks even more spirit, less flesh and blood. We wander,
holding our moments, her arm in mine.

We grin at the cheeky banter of the vendors, muscled men, likely
descended from slaves who grew strong on black beans like the ones

heaped up in these bins. *Feijoada*, Brazil's national dish, Dona Lurdes explains, was the sustaining soul food of slaves—black beans flavoured with *rabo salgado*, salty pig's tails, the only bit of the beast nobody wanted. The men twirl plastic bags of produce, call to us, "Saco cheio, saco cheio"—Fill your bag, fill your bag, which isn't funny until you know Brazilian slang. "Saco cheio" also means "my testicles are full" and both men and women curse this way when it is time to say they have had it, right up to here, with this shit.

A passing man motions to the vendors, yells, "O meio saco esta cheio ja!"—My bag is already full, which is to say, I've already had enough shit, and everyone laughs out loud. I laugh more to think that this market is called the *Sacolão*, the big sack.

Dona Lurdes sees I'm amused, says, "Você fala português, ne?" proud of her protégé.

I too feel pleased, and I watch Dona Lurdes shop in her neat, careful way, quick fingers turning the oranges over and over, placing them back just so, just like her son, my husband, does as he engages Italian widows back home on St. Clair Avenue, discussing tomato quality, fresh greens.

Yes, I do speak the language—thanks to her, like a woman in her sixties from the south of Brazil. Like her, I say *chemia*, not *geleia*, when I mean jam. The city dwellers howl with laughter as it trips out of my mouth, try to get their heads around what this *gringa* in São Paulo could possibly be saying.

I practice pronouncing *jabuticaba* as we buy the unfamiliar fruit, dark purple, like a wild grape. Dona Lurdes shows me how to hold the melons—tucked into your side like a football—to prevent thieves from snatching them and running. She's always translating "os jeitos do Brasil"—the ways of Brazil.

She buys an extra loaf of bread, which we deliver on the way home. At the foot of a tree near the busy viaduct, she stops and calls up, "Tem alguém em casa?"—Is anyone home? A street kid with matted hair perches on a branch above us. He smiles and reaches for the bread. They make small talk and Dona Lurdes teases him, says all he needs now is an exercise bike to be right at home. The kid, she explains as we walk on, lives in a tree because it's safer than being on the ground.

Dona Lurdes makes rounds to give food to the homeless. Her six daughters all chide her for giving away the groceries, but they don't mean it, remember how it is to be hungry. Back in Rio Grande do Sul, Dona Lurdes had raised eight children. No running water, no electricity, and at times, no roof for shelter. Her husband, Osvaldo, was away a lot driving a truck. Back then, Dona Lurdes would sometimes rise before dawn to sew and then go door-to-door to sell her work. If someone bought, there would be bread and milk for breakfast.

Now, times are good. Inez, a successful executive at a small manufacturing firm, brought her mother to São Paulo to give her an easy life. "Did I tell you I'm going to join an amateur theatre?" Dona Lurdes asks as we walk slowly uphill to Inez's house. Her blue eyes shine. She's always wanted to be on the stage. As she unlocks the wrought-iron front gate she adds, "After that I'm going to start a sewing business." I don't know what to say. Hope—or denial?

Late that afternoon after our siesta, I hear the phone ring. Dona Lurdes answers. I eavesdrop. Wrong number—yet she keeps chatting. In a city of twenty million people, and despite the household's recent move to a new residence with a new phone number, the caller is someone Dona Lurdes knows. She has recognized the voice of the brother of Inez's ex-boyfriend. I hear her explain her situation, ask if he could drive her out to Ipiranga.

And so it transpires that before sundown, undetected by Inez, Dona Lurdes has secured passage to see Dr. Fritz, who is performing miracles across town.

That evening, Antonio explains the strange legend of "Dr. Fritz," well known to Brazilians. Adolf Frederick Yeperssoven was a German physician who died in a World War I field hospital. Apparently he hadn't yet finished his work on earth, so ever since his death, his soul has travelled across the Atlantic Ocean to the southern hemisphere to inhabit Brazilian men, who then become faith healers.

The first and most famous of these, Antonio tells me, was Zé Arigó, a peasant and Brazilian psychic surgeon who in 1948 started using kitchen knives and pocket blades to operate while in a trance, and who invoked Jesus to stop the bleeding. Known as "the surgeon of the rusty knife," he went from being a poor nobody to a celebrated and wealthy man before he died in a car crash in 1971.

I'd heard of Zé Arigó at a seminar about Brazil at the University of Toronto. The lecturer, a Canadian doctor who had seen the faith healer at work, showed us photos, and to my surprise, was not the least bit dismissive. "There are some things you just can't explain" was the upshot of his talk.

Intrigued, I'd done some research and found that Dr. Fritz didn't shun the medical establishment. He welcomed them to study his unorthodox methods, and many films and TV programs document his procedures. His "surgeries" are characterized by little blood, no pain for patients, and no infection, even when he dislodges a bullet from near the spine by whacking away in a hammer-and-chisel action to get his dull knives to cut, or when he digs scissors or fingers into the vertebra of a paraplegic, or cuts into someone to remove a tumour. It's something even Dr. Fritz can't explain. It's from God, he told interviewers, and people of faith can heal themselves.

A *Publishers Weekly* review of a book about Zé Arigó from 1974 echoed the respectful tone of the physician's lecture at the University of Toronto. "How Arigó did what he did remains a subject for wonder and conjecture," wrote the reviewer. "That he was a psychic healer of phenomenal powers the reader of this well-documented study will hardly doubt."

This esteemed incarnation of "Dr. Fritz" was followed by others: the improbably named Oscar Wilde, who died in a car accident, and his brother Edvaldo, also killed in a crash, and most notably, Edson Queiroz, a gynaecologist in Recife, who died after being stabbed to death by a staff member in 1991. Dr. Fritz, legend holds, always comes to a violent end. At one point, a journalist had interviewed Dr. Fritz while he was still in Queiroz's body. The doctor had insisted that he was in his final incarnation.

Undeterred, the current Dr. Fritz, Rubens Faria Jr., an electrical engineer from Rio, claimed to be Dr. Fritz as early as 1986, even before the doctor's previous incarnation was dead. In recent years, this Dr. Fritz had been "treating" more than 5,000 people each week in Rio de Janeiro and São Paulo. All classes, races, and nationalities are drawn to Dr. Fritz, Antonio tells me, not only the poor. Superman actor Christopher Reeve is reportedly among those who tried the "psychic surgery."

Brazil's idiosyncratic spiritual traditions never fail to confuse me. The Pope, people joke, is so exasperated by widespread syncretic beliefs that, even though Brazil has the world's largest Roman Catholic population, he wants to excommunicate the whole country. Here, Catholicism is spiced with everything from African religions such as candomblé, with its healing, music, dance, and spirit possession; to Native shamanism; to Protestant evangelism; to mystical "spiritist" cults, notably one from France based on the nineteenth-century work of Allan Kardec—which is, as far as I can tell, where faith healing and Dr. Fritz come in.

Dona Lurdes is Catholic. She has a shrine in her bedroom, adorned with a statue of Our Lady of Lourdes and fresh flowers. So why does she want to visit a faith healer, an activity that's definitely not sanctioned by her church?

I know this all falls under what Antonio calls, "Only in Brazil," when I press him for more rational explanations. But the Dr. Fritz phenomenon seems extra baffling to me.

"How can anyone believe in this?" I finally ask.

Antonio shrugs. "Sometimes it's all people have left," he replies, his face sad.

We decide we will accompany Dona Lurdes tomorrow.

After Inez departs for work the next morning, our ride arrives. He's pudgy, Japanese—and believes in the power of Dr. Fritz. We travel for two hours, still within the sprawling city limits. We finally arrive in Ipiranga, which in native Tupi-Guarani means "red river." I think of the flowing radiation lines on Dona Lurdes's chest. We shake hands with her Charon, who wants no coin to pay for passage, tells us he is simply happy to help. "Believe in God and trust in Dr. Fritz," he calls as he drives off.

Through the crowded streets we walk until we reach an old warehouse. The entrance is a hole in a crumbling wall. We step over fallen bricks, and just inside there's a table covered with plastic pill cups, each filled with green liquid. A handwritten sign proclaims that this medical miracle can help you throw away your cigarettes forever. Smoking is bad for unborn children, the warning goes, and to illustrate, a damaged fetus floats in a large bottle. A hugely pregnant woman, who is smoking, downs a shot of the green liquid, shrugs, and laughs with the vendor.

We pay the equivalent of twenty American dollars—a vast sum for the average Brazilian—to rude people at a wicket. Behind them is what is left of a building: on the ground floor a couple of big rooms, and stairs going up to more rooms on the second floor.

We join hundreds of others to sit in the disintegrating lot. People— blind, disabled, the terminally ill—perch on corners of old brick walls, amid the rubble of scattered bricks and litter, or squat on the sun-baked earth. There are no chairs, except wheelchairs, no trees or plants. So many sick people, so much suffering. But everyone is patient.

A woman of about twenty-five who sits on the ground beside us begins to talk about all she's going to do once she's cured. "I'm going to climb a tree, for one thing," she declares. "And dance until dawn." She is cheerful despite the bandages over both of her eyes. She says she's been losing her sight for years, but that Dr. Fritz gives her hope.

Brazilian belief in the mysterious power of unseen forces always amazes me. Here, hundreds of patients line up, often waiting from early morning until almost midnight for treatment. Prior to his marathon treatment sessions, Farias is said to enter into a trance from which he emerges as the German-speaking Dr. Fritz. That a spirit can possess a living person is simply a given.

All that day sitting in the dirt in the hot sun, Dona Lurdes doesn't eat, and we have to convince her to even drink something. There is no food available except popcorn. She rarely speaks, has gone inward. I think she's praying. I'm thankful that Dona Lurdes is not here alone. After eight hours, it is our time to begin lining up. Two hours later, we are still shuffling slowly forward. It's early evening when I notice the air is charged with a new energy.

The man ahead of us points out Dr. Fritz's wife, Rita Costa. She's blond, in a black dress and heels, very up-market despite her white lab coat, like she's ready for a gala. A clique of blond, pretty assistants talking into cell phones. Like runway models, they parade up and down, begin to usher rich people down a central path that leads to the stairs to the second-floor.

That, the man in line adds, is where Dr. Fritz performs surgery. "Surgery" with dull knives, scissors, and hypodermic needles, Antonio says, and no anesthesia or sterilization. The key is faith, in order to heal the astral body as well as the physical body. I'm familiar with the idea of an "energy body," described in yoga, or the meridian theory of acupuncture or shiatsu. Many scientific studies have found that positive thinking and prayer can heal. But why, if Dr. Fritz has such power, does he need to perform invasive surgery with blunt, dirty instruments?

Now, I watch two muscular men half-carry another man with a knife sticking out of his back up the stairs to Dr. Fritz's "surgery." Antonio says one of the men is holding the knife in place. Pure theatre. A limping old man with expensive clothes and a cane—I call him the Admiral—is escorted right between the lines of poor people who have been waiting all day. Fuming, I glance around. No one looks resentful. On the contrary, the people in line appear to be enjoying the spectacle.

Eventually, we arrive in the big ground-floor room, from which we will move to the smaller waiting room, and then out to the front where Dr. Fritz will treat people. It's been a total of twelve hours of waiting: in line four hours, after eight hours of sitting. There has been no complaint from Dona Lurdes. I'm thirty-seven, healthy, and completely worn out.

A huge, officious black man in expensive leather shoes says, "Move over here, sister." His fake-pious voice unleashes a wave of violence in me. I notice many men like him here inside. They are beefy, well dressed, polite, and vaguely menacing. Security, I realize.

As we move forward, they begin shoving people roughly through the narrow doors into the smaller waiting room, packing us in. It's pandemonium. Antonio holds tightly to his mother and me. Suddenly, a young man, possibly schizophrenic, starts yelling incoherently and fighting. The security men grab him in a practiced motion and carry him off.

"He has the devil in him," someone shouts. Dozens of people fall on their knees and recite a prayer, eyes closed: "Avé Maria, cheia de graça, o Senhor é convosco... bendito é o fruto do vosso ventre, Jesus. Santa Maria, mãe de Deus...agora e na hora da nossa morte." Never anger, always prayer, even here, even in "the hour of our death." We struggle toward the few chairs in the room, and for Dona Lurdes, so obviously unwell, someone gets up. It's midnight by the time we emerge from this corral to join the last line, where we can finally see the show, become part of it.

Dona Lurdes stands, X-ray in hand, her thin chest marked with the red river of lines. She looks energized, hopeful. We step out of the line and stand nearby. I see Dr. Fritz for the first time. He's short, about forty, and frenzied. His face is angry, and he's shouting in *Hogan's Heroes* accented Portuguese. "Shut up! If you don't shut up, I'll leave. Remain silent, and trust in God."

Dona Lurdes murmurs, "See, that's his German side." Apparently, Doctor Fritz is an ill-humoured German with perfect vision. Everyone knows when the doctor is in: the new accent, the rudeness, and when the myopic Rubens throws away his glasses.

Dr. Fritz moves down the line, spending a few seconds with each person. He appears to be giving injections and then throwing the cotton balls into a bin carried by his wife. I try to see clearly. It looks like he's squirting whatever fluid is in the syringe—an iodine solution, it's rumoured—into the cotton ball, not into the people. Then it does appear that he injects someone's eye—I see it from the side. The person doesn't flinch, looks rapturously at Dr. Fritz. For a moment I want it to be true.

When he arrives at Dona Lurdes, she waves the X-ray, asks him for a little more than the injection. He barely pauses at the tiny, frail woman. In that moment, Dr. Fritz stops, and turns around and looks at us. For an instant he is caught in the ray of Antonio's one-pointed hatred—before he moves on to the next person.

Dona Lurdes got less than ten seconds for her money, her faith, and a whole day and night out of her dwindling time on earth.

Antonio is scarily mild over his rage. He holds his mother's arm as we leave the collapsing compound. We live so far from here, and it's unsafe to be out on the *Blade Runner* streets at night. We are terrified of being assaulted. Before that can happen, we find a cab. But our driver doesn't know the way back. He speeds toward no destination, and we finally exhale only when he transfers us to another driver who knows our way home.

The hot, dirty, urban blight of São Paulo, yet how beautiful it looks at night. We make our way over a river—the Ipiranga, red river? The water is a dark gap in the disorder of stars.

"Dr. Fritz said to trust in God." Dona Lurdes's voice is reverent. "The Lord's hand was there." She sinks back into the soft seat and blessedly, falls asleep.

It's four in the morning when we arrive back in Alto da Lapa. Inez hears us come in and runs downstairs. "Are you insane?" she yells. "You took her there?"

"What, we should have let her go by herself?" Antonio replies softly.

"Please, I feel much better now," Dona Lurdes protests. Her face is haggard, yet peaceful. Expectant almost. It dawns on me—she trusts that she's been healed. Her hope for salvation: all she's got left.

Inez, quiet now, begins to help her mother upstairs to bed. I think of Our Lady of Lourdes, wonder whether Dona Lurdes will pray now to the little shrine in her room. Millions of pilgrims go to France each year, hoping for physical or spiritual healing in the grotto's sacred waters, where miracles occur. Can faith cure illness? Can energy heal?

Dona Lurdes believes it can. She trusts in the faith healer. So I let myself hope.

The Unholy Yogi

IN THE BUSY PORT OF NASSAU, I SLIP THROUGH A GAP IN THE chain-link fence and walk toward some industrial warehouses. Squeaky cranes move shipping containers on and off cargo ships, and this has to be the wrong place. Then I spot a tiny pastel-painted sign decorated with lotus flowers, butterflies, and people doing headstands: Sivananda Ashram Yoga Retreat. Mermaid Dock. I sit on a bench to wait for the boat that will transport me to Paradise Island. Blue Bahamian water shines in the sunlight and dazzles my winter-weary eyes. Off the edge of the pier, discarded conch shells by the hundreds tint the depths a delicate pinky-cream.

A sudden thump startles me, and I turn to see an athletic, agitated woman with a sparkly diamond nose stud rummaging through a backpack on the ground. She pulls out a smoke, lights it with a metal Zippo, and closes her eyes, inhaling deeply. About half the cigarette is gone, the empty pack still crumpled in her hand, before she glances up and notices me, clutching my latte and observing her.

"Where'd you get that?" she asks.

"Two blocks," I point.

I feel like asking her for a cigarette. I haven't smoked in years. It's my reforming-hedonist reflex kicking in, which happens whenever I'm faced with prohibition. At yoga school, there will be no tobacco—or any other "intoxicants."

"Want to walk with me to get coffee?" she asks.

We glance across the water. No boats, so we grab our bags and head back onto Bay Street. Her name is Polly and she's a yoga teacher already, here for more training. I love her New York accent, how she says everything is "ex-straw-din-ary." She's in her thirties, a cult queen back in Williamsburg, involved in the art and music scenes. She lives in a renovated sugar factory loft near the end of the Brooklyn Bridge with her boyfriend, a computer geek. I tell her I'd recently moved with my husband to a small Canadian university town, where I plan to teach yoga and lead a quieter, more artistic life.

Polly walks and talks fast. We each buy and slurp down an Americano, then, even though it's morning, go on the hunt for ice cream. Two chocolate-laced double-scoops later, she vibrates and the roots of my hair stand up. As we power-walk back to the dock we make a solemn pact that on our day off next week, we'll go to town together to eat forbidden seafood and drink forbidden wine.

Polly bums a cigarette from a dockworker. He smiles broadly, sways to a calypso beat that blasts from his radio, and unrolls the pack from his T-shirt sleeve. Polly lights up and starts to smoke the way people do when they're about to quit. Inhaling deeply, cheeks hollowing out. "We should start to diarize our transgressions," she says between puffs. "Uh oh," she adds, pointing at a boat speeding our way. Three quick drags and she grinds the cigarette under her heel.

And so we embark. For the whole month of February at yoga school, we must commit to no tobacco, caffeine, alcohol, drugs, eggs, meat, fowl, fish. Not even garlic or onions, which apparently make one "rajasic," creating agitation in meditation. For me, worst of all is no wine. I'm here, I remind myself, because I'm tired of my own excesses and have resolved to try something new: abstinence, vegetarian food, just two meals and four hours of yoga each day. Polly, who smokes a pack a day, looks as edgy as I feel. We climb aboard the tossing boat. "What are we doing here?" I ask. She laughs and mimics jumping overboard.

That afternoon in the ashram's shop, I flip through page after page of photographs of a small Indian man in a Speedo performing yoga poses. "Where did they find this hairy guy?" I ask the blond woman behind the counter. She looks up, brown eyes amused.

"I mean, he's really advanced," I say, holding the book out to show hairy man in scorpion pose, balanced on his forearms, his back arched so his feet touch his head. "But couldn't they have found a more attractive model?"

"That's Swami Vishnu Devananda," she responds.

"Oh," I say sheepishly. We exchange grins as I slide the *Complete Illustrated Book of Yoga* across the counter. This will be my main textbook for the next month here at Swami Vishnu's school. Just arrived, and already I've dissed the guru.

"I guess I have a lot to learn."

"Don't worry, I came here thinking it was a spa," she gives a wicked laugh. "I unpacked and asked, 'Where's the bar?' That was my old life." Waving a tanned hand as though to say, "eons ago," she tells me her name is Mahadevi. For the past five years, she's lived on the ashram's five acres, between the bay and the deep blue sea.

"Why have you come here?" she asks, handing me the second required text, a 600-page copy of the *Bhagavad Gita*.

"I want to learn to teach yoga," I say, handing her my money. "It makes me peaceful, and I'd like to share that." I don't mention my vague hope of escaping ingrained habits and stultifying routines, or of finding a healthier, congruent life. I've been doing yoga for years, I tell her, but know little about ashrams or about yoga's wider framework beyond the *asanas*, the physical postures. "I'm curious, but clueless," I shrug.

"That's how I was too," Mahadevi says. "I'd never have believed I'd end up living here." People at the ashram go by their spiritual names, so the place is full of Mahadevis and other characters from Indian mythology, she explains. As she tells her story, I try to imagine her as a Greek-American divorced inebriate named Eleni, demanding martinis. I fail. Her hair gleams gold, her skin is sun-burnished. Her face and manner are open. She looks incredibly healthy and content.

Relief floods me as she talks. I'd heard that Sivananda yoga teacher training, as well as being thorough, was very "spiritual." This had conjured nightmares of being marooned on an island of holy-roller yogis for a month. It's been three hours since I arrived on the ashram's boat, and already I've found the subversive element: a yoga teacher who smokes, and now, an accidental yogi.

The path is fringed with ferns, green foliage, and tropical flowers—red, orange, pink, and white hibiscuses, and bougainvillea—and lithe palm trees. Sure beats Kingston, Ontario, in February. As I explore, Tony Bennett croons in my head, "Take my hand, I'm a stranger in paradise." The absurdity of this soundtrack pleases me. A large sign with the heart chakra painted on it proclaims, "God is one. The names are many," and beneath, "The highest religion is love." I roll my eyes, and smile too.

My uniforms and the teacher-training manual are waiting at the nearby office. Both have an image of Swami Vishnu on the front. This time, he's doing a lunge. He's so flexible that his back leg, spine, and arms form a semi-circle. Swami Vishnu was the student of Swami Sivananda of Rishikesh, India, whom he named his yoga schools after. The ocean is a short walk farther on. Today, it's a calm turquoise line between white sand and blue sky. On the beachside yoga platform encircled by palms, I sigh with happiness. It's more beautiful than any place I've seen, or imagined, to do yoga. Humming "All lost in a wonderland," I walk by the kitchen and outdoor dining area and head back toward the bay side of the ashram.

I pass the office, the garden yoga platform, and the shop. At its adjoining Health Hut, you can sit and have tea, or even ice cream, at certain hours. It's a small concession to sugar by the ashram, likely to prevent mutiny by junk-food-deprived yoga students who might otherwise decide to swim in desperation to shore.

I meander past the main temple and the dock, where the ashram's boat is disgorging more teacher trainees. There's also a houseboat where the teachers live and a cabana that was Swami Vishnu's when he was alive. Nearby is my tent, which I'd pitched earlier on a windy point beside a small clump of trees. In this spot, lush vegetation has given way to bare earth, denuded by the many shelters erected here during teacher training courses.

Now, a second tent huddles next to mine on the otherwise empty campground. A skinny young woman with long curly brown hair, tight jeans, and clunky high heels stands next to it. She's trembling, looking back and forth from her tiny tent to her two huge suitcases. When she sees me she wails, "How can I make it fit?"

Her name is Ilana, she sniffles, and she's just arrived from Tel Aviv. She slumps down, waiflike, on a suitcase. I suggest that the administrators might have a bigger tent. She brightens when I remind her that the senior teachers here are also from Israel. I hand her the uniforms I'm holding: two T-shirts, yellow, the colour of spiritual aspiration, each sporting Swami Vishnu's picture and a crest that says "Unity in Diversity," plus two pairs of baggy white cotton drawstring pants. "Check these out. We have to wear them most of the time," I tell her. The outfit is to identify us to the community as Teacher Training Course students. She looks horrified, even more so when I say she can always store her suitcases because she won't need her other clothes. I feel an odd pleasure at her discomfiture, at how silly she is, and unprepared.

Not very yogic, I think, and to redeem myself, I offer to watch her bags while she goes to seek help. My own Canadian-Tire-special tent has just enough room for a blow-up mattress and my knapsack, leaving a tiny square to crouch in while getting in and out of bed, so I don't know why I'm being smug. In the busy channel between the campground and the mainland, cargo ships glide silently to and from the docklands, expensive yachts proliferate like seagulls, and floatplanes take off and land in the water-gaps between vessels.

A powerboat roars up. As it nears the campground, someone cuts the engines. On board, a man talks into a megaphone. "This here is the Port of Nassau folks," he says, waving his hand. The deck is crowded, and everyone holds a cocktail. A tour group?

"And this here is a yoga ash-ram," he continues, separating the word in two. "They don't eat meat, they don't drink, and they don't have sex." A calculated pause, and then: "Guess they ain't our kinda people!" The tourists all shout, "Hell no!" As the boat's engine revs and they speed away, cocktails aloft, I contemplate a goblet of fruity Tempranillo and wonder—not for the last time—whether I'm on the wrong side.

Next morning, the yoga teacher training course begins. It's still dark when the five thirty bell rings. I stagger outside as Ilana emerges from her palatial new tent, borrowed from her country people. We're both exhausted. All night, squawking cranes loaded and unloaded shipping containers just across the bay, while music blasted from nearby resorts and the city-sized cruise ships docked in Nassau.

We head for the bathhouse. People stand at a row of outdoor sinks brushing their teeth, and, in case we'd forgotten where we are, using neti pots. Heads tilted to one side, they pour salt water in one nostril and let it stream out the other. We hurry back to the tents to pull on our uniforms and rush to the temple for six o'clock *satsang*. Seventy of us arrive at once, marked as teacher trainees by our yellow T-shirts and white pants.

Inside the temple, we sit in silent meditation for a half hour. So begins our introduction to the routine we'll follow for the next twenty-eight days. Wherever you are in the world, Sivananda yoga ashrams—of which there are nine, plus many smaller centres—follow the same 5:30 a.m. to 10:30 p.m. timetable. I'd read somewhere that the idea of the intense schedule is to purify students through the path of yoga so they may reach god consciousness—whatever that means. A Sunday school dropout, I liked the practical website blurb better. "The teacher training course is a profound personal experience, designed to build a firm foundation of inner discipline and provide the proficiency to teach others."

Surreptitiously, I spend the whole thirty-minute meditation looking around. Everyone else sits eerily still. The temple is plain, but graceful. Up front is a small altar, and around it, pictures of deities such as a blue guy and a monkey god; a photo of Swami Sivananda, who looks like a kindly Dr. Evil, and one of his devoted students, Swami Vishnu—round face, dazzling smile, air of mischief. Swami Vishnu was born in Kerala in 1927, our training manual said, and died in 1993. When he was just eighteen he'd met Swami Sivananda in India, and was later sent to the West by his master with ten rupees in his pocket and the encouragement, "People are waiting."

I try to imagine Swami Vishnu's arrival in Montreal in 1959 as one of Canada's first yoga teachers. A small brown man in orange robes who promoted strange acrobatics, he must have seemed extravagantly weird, even dangerous. Somehow, with little money or English, he started a yoga school in Montreal. Later he founded what would become international

Sivananda headquarters in Val Morin, Quebec, in the Laurentian Mountains, and eventually, ashrams and centres around the world.

When the harmonium drones to life my mind returns from wandering, and the daily call-and-response chants, *kirtan*, begin. I resist chanting *Jaya Ganesha*—Hail Ganesha, the elephant god—and songs in Sanskrit and English and Hebrew from our books. It seems dorky. Around me, people sway and clap along, except for many tense-looking yoga teacher trainees.

"Chanting is an exercise in concentration and a way of opening the heart and experiencing joy," explains our senior teacher in the lecture that follows. He bears an unfortunate resemblance to Peter Sellers with a beard. "Chanting relates to *bhakti* yoga," he adds, "the yoga of love and devotion, which appeals to people with emotional natures." At the end of *satsang* there's a final chant, during which a plump Brahmin priest rings a bell and waves a flame. As we leave the temple, a woman in white offers everyone a slice of apple from a tray. We skirmish for our lost shoes and run to make it to the eight o'clock yoga *asana* class on the garden platform.

The familiar yoga sequence of movements—which I'd learned in Toronto from a teacher trained in the Sivananda tradition—feels like a relief, reminds me of why I'm here. We begin each class with an unpronounceable Sanskrit chant then do two breathing practices: breath of fire and alternate nostril breathing. Then sun salutations and variations on twelve *asanas*: headstand, shoulderstand, plough, fish, seated forward bend, cobra, locust, bow, spinal twist, crow, standing forward bend, triangle. At the end, we sink into relaxation, integrating the effects of our two-hour practice.

I'm always struck by the simplicity and elegance of yoga. "Health is wealth. Peace is happiness. Yoga shows the way," Swami Vishnu had written. Yes, I'd thought. I like the yogic concept of "born divine"—the opposite of the "born doomed" of my Hebridean ancestors. I'm also curious about the dissonance between yoga's "woo-woo" reputation and its practicality. You do the movements and breathing exercises, and you experience the benefits. Simple. This, I'm told, leads students naturally toward yoga's fuller spiritual and philosophical path.

When it's time for brunch at ten o'clock we're all famished. People line up at long outdoor tables full of food. I fill my plate and ladle herbal tea out of a giant pot. At one of the communal tables I wolf down homemade bread with peanut butter and jam, craving coffee but otherwise happy. Where else can you meditate in a temple, chant, join a ceremony led by a tantric priest, and do yoga—all before breakfast?

A tanned man in yellow clothes sits down beside me. He is exceedingly good-looking. His name is Omkara, he says; he's from Israel, and he's a *brahmacharya*—whatever that means.

"You are enjoying that?" he asks, watching me scoff the bread.

"Yes, it's really good."

"But is it good, or is it pleasant?" he says with mischief in his eyes.

"Uh—pardon?"

"Good, or pleasant?" He sees my puzzled look. "Don't worry, soon you'll know the difference," he adds in a brotherly tone.

He doesn't respond when teacher trainees at our table begin to complain. "I feel like I'm in Bahamas, India," a tattooed woman sniffs. She's angry at being asked to cover her knees and shoulders. Others object to the religious rituals of the temple. "A bunch of North Americans playing Hindu," one sneers. Personally, I don't like chanting—there's something so wholesome about it. But I'm glad to participate in meaningful rituals full of light, flowers, incense, and music, and to deepen my yoga knowledge. Aside from the pure sensual pleasure, I'm interested to learn about deities, which symbolize aspects of our consciousness, and how *Surya Namaskar*, the sun salutation sequence, is named for the Hindu sun god, Surya. Anyway, whether yoga grew from India's soil alongside Hinduism or not, as some modern-day historians argue, yoga is a universal path, "the great divine soul penetrates all," etcetera. So what's the problem?

At noon, we teacher trainees gather in the temple for a lecture on the *Bhagavad Gita*. It's a section of an epic poem, the *Mahabharata*, and an essential yoga scripture. After this lecture ends, the day folds back on itself: another lecture, yoga again, evening meal at six o'clock, and then back to the temple. About two hundred people, trainees, residents, teachers, and guests, descend for evening *satsang* at eight o'clock. We line up again for attendance, a new feature of our lives that, along with the uniforms and all the rules, makes us feel like schoolchildren.

On the temple floor, which seems to get harder and harder, we sit for meditation. There's a millisecond of peace before a familiar guitar riff twangs across the bay: "Sweet Home Alabama. Where skies are blue…" I attempt to draw my awareness inward to my breath while the cruise ship's disco obliterates half an hour of silence—as it does every night for the next twenty-eight nights.

The harmonium wheezes, signalling that chanting will begin. Everyone sings and plays instruments and looks devotional—teachers in orange robes, *brahmacharya* in yellow. The latter, I've learned, are in training to be teachers and are celibate. The idea is to sublimate sexual energy into spiritual energy to use for meditation. A young blond man in yellow named Gopala is asked to lead the call-and-response chanting. All the young women lean toward him, magnetized by the passion in his voice and his angelic good looks. From what I see, he must be the world's most challenged *brahmacharya*.

We repeat the closing fire ritual, called *arati*, as in the morning. The priest waves flames before an altar, representing the removal of darkness by the bestowal of divine light. There's something primal about it. It's a traditional Hindu ceremony, my book explained, relating to the false and the real self. Lighting the oil lamps also denotes the melting of ego. We chant a singularly beautiful mantra together—"Twameva mata, cha pita twameva"—and the priest turns and offers us the flame. We hold up our palms as though catching the light and draw it over our eyes and our bodies, as you might with sweetgrass. A tray of *prasad* awaits us on the way out, fruits or sweets blessed with the vibrations of our meditation, prayer, and chanting. Then the shoe skirmish is repeated.

It's ten thirty and I'm dog-tired. I stop at the shop to ask Mahadevi if she sells earplugs, anticipating another night of noisy container ships and club music. She says no and assures me, inexplicably, that I won't need them anyway. I wish her a good night and stagger through the enfolding darkness to my tent. I flop down on my air mattress, certain I'll be awake until dawn. Awash in the day's sensory pleasures—flowers, fruit, sunlight, fresh air, music, limitless blue ocean—I drift off and blessedly, fall asleep.

The next day, we receive our "karma yoga" assignments. Doing an hour of daily "selfless service" is meant to help students "eliminate egoistic and selfish tendencies." Now we *really* have no time. I pray not to work in the kitchen because I'm too attached to food. Sure enough, my duty is to wash up after brunch. When Ken, the man who manages the kitchen, points out where leftovers are kept, I curse inwardly. My tendency is always to eat, drink, and be merry. Lately, I've been realizing that this is unsustainable for good health. Plus I'm bored by my own excessive habits. I've resolved to try new ones here.

Washing pots after brunch with other karma yogis, two Irish and two American women, I join in mild gossip. Our favourite topics are the dark-haired British model with a drug problem who hands out Sai Baba cards, the American son of a scion who has never rinsed his own dishes before, and the bendy young narcissist from Vancouver whom we mock for her vegan shoes. We also talk about the sexy tabla player with the strong arms who has just arrived from the States, his wild energy a welcome tonic for the off-key chanting of the "Garden Swami," who, we all agree, tends the grounds far better than she sings. Frequently, we talk about everyone's favourite *brahmacharya*, Gopala.

Mainly, however, we just scrub institutional-sized vessels and try to learn the twenty-five-line *Gajananam* in Sanskrit. It's rumoured we have to recite the whole mantra, with eight devilish lines in the middle about inertness and laziness that I *cannot* remember, in order to graduate.

The whole first week is gruelling, like an endurance test. A Greek guy says his army service was much easier. Alice, one of the Irishwomen I scrub pots with, says she sometimes feels like she's in prison. "No, prison is nicer," she corrects herself, giving a massive soup tureen some elbow grease. "You don't have to get up at five thirty, and you get coffee and three meals a day."

In the evenings especially, I obsess about the taste of Tempranillo sipped out of a globe-shaped goblet. Or crunchy melted sugar with the soft yellow custard of a crème brulée. In this way I revisit much of the wine and food of Spain. Even the utilitarian, Indian-style contents of the leftovers fridge pose a constant temptation. My stomach rumbles. I long for espresso and cappuccino and Americano and latte. I'd chew plain coffee beans if I only had some.

My head splitting from coffee deficiency, I visit Mahadevi. She suggests the judicious use of chocolate kisses. "Only buy as many as you need," she says. I take most of what she's got.

The week, despite its privations, feels satisfying. I'm starting to move, and breathe, easily. It's amazing how much happens in twenty-four hours here, and I like what we're learning. This includes yoga *asanas* and how to teach them to students at different levels, breathing practices, *bandhas* (energy locks) and *kriyas* (purification practices), meditation, karma and reincarnation, and yoga scriptures. How could anyone not be fascinated by these explorations into consciousness, the body, freedom, the nature of reality? Western society always gives the mind primacy, and I find the yogic view fascinating. It's along the lines of what Rainer Maria Rilke wrote in *Letters to a Young Poet*: "Intellectual creation too springs from the physical."

But many people are already deeply unhappy.

Toward the end of the week, a likeable man who has taught our yoga class a few times, Vijaya, tells us about his difficult early days at the ashram. We're all ears. He's a long-time Sivananda teacher and one of the teacher-trainee-course counsellors, all volunteers here to help any student who has issues. In the sixties when he first arrived in Paradise Island, he says, he was a wild young guy who didn't like anyone telling him anything. He'd done some transcendental meditation, but not much. When he realized he'd be meditating in a temple and singing devotional songs with a priest doing rituals with flowers and flames, he wanted out.

"One problem: I didn't have enough money to change my airline ticket," he recalls. "I was stuck here."

His rocky start, he says, was just the beginning of years in conflict with Swami Vishnu. "My karma yoga was to build a six-foot sea wall, and life continued like that," Vijaya says wryly. He blames this on his own wrong-headedness. He speaks of "Swamiji"—who is variously described as sweet, funny, confident, mercurial, tough, and dictatorial—with great affection.

He tells us how our teacher-trainee course is going to be. The first week, he says, we'll feel adrenaline and energy in the air. The second week, people will get tired. And the third week, the food and postures will have changed us, our egos will kick up to put on the brakes, and people will quit. He doesn't say anything about the fourth week.

"The course can be really hard," he cautions. "But I advise you to stick it out and see what happens." He adds emphatically, "Yoga philosophy asks you not to believe someone else, but to explore for yourself and then decide."

I like this. I'm a natural mocker, and skepticism has long been my default. But lately I've been starting to feel that it's the easy way out, a lack of discernment: be aloof, think you're smart because you're not being credulous. And stay the same forever. Maybe life is like a movie. You have to suspend your disbelief or you can't enjoy the show. Otherwise, how can you decide what experiences are worth your time? Judging at the outset kills all possibility for new inspirations and ideas. Now I want to try things, even ostensibly crazy things. Like doing acid as a teenager—you need to find ways to rearrange your brain sometimes so new and strange connections can be made.

"Who knows," Vijaya says with a grin, "you too may be surprised to find yourself, twenty-two years later, teaching at the ashram you were so desperate to escape."

During the question period, someone asks him what he thinks now about *kirtan*. Sanskrit mantras are "energy encased in a sound structure" that represent aspects of the divine, and we can tune in to these, he says.

"Chants put divine positive energy in your head, which is better than your usual chattering mind radio," he adds. Does he know about Tony Bennett—"Won't you answer the fervent prayer of a stranger in paradise"—looping endlessly in my head?

As a small experiment, I resolve to drop my judgments about chanting in the temple and see how that goes.

The next day, Friday, is our day "off." This means we only have to be at the temple from six to eight in the morning and six to eight in the evening, and also do our karma yoga. Mine is right after brunch around eleven o'clock, so it cuts my day in half. Polly and I both decide we don't want to go transgress on the mainland anyway. We vow to swear and slouch, and maybe swim, instead.

Polly, so electrically hyper that I suspect she plugs herself in at night, says she's bored. She does admit to enjoying the beauty of this place, and the anthropologically remarkable people from many parts of the world who include models, engineers, lawyers, financial wizards, aging hippies, biodynamic farmers, psychiatrists, psychics, fitness instructors, musicians, and artists of all kinds. After morning *satsang*, Ilana, an economist back in Tel Aviv, calls me over to show off her latest acquisition. The Israelis are indulging her, I think, envious. I sometimes feel spiteful toward people who I sense are used to comfort and wealth. Her tent is so big we can stand up inside, and she demonstrates her new shelf, adorned with books, artfully draped sarongs, and even framed photographs.

"We're just like Uwe and Gustav," I say. I tell her the story of *Enlightenment Guaranteed*, a German film in which two brothers try to sort out the mess of their lives by going to a Japanese monastery. Before they get there, in Tokyo, they lose their belongings and identities—and then, one another. Uwe has a food fetish. Stripped of everything, he goes into a sushi restaurant, fills his face, and then runs. Gustav, fixated on shelter, steals a tent from a camping store and climbs in. I look at Ilana's sultan's palace and confess to her about the magnetic pull the leftovers fridge exerts on me.

We laugh and agree it's weird how we re-manifest what's familiar in our lives, even when we start from zero. Conditioning. Maybe yoga really can help us to see beyond this, to look under the surface, investigate the human condition, and its impermanence and suffering, as the swamis, our teachers, have been telling us.

Or maybe not. The campground is crowded with happy, off-duty students eating illicit junk from the mainland, lazing and generally reverting to normal behaviour. The tour boat slows down out in the bay. "Okay, lovebirds, this here is the yoga ashram." It's a different megaphone man. "They don't eat meat, they don't drink, and they don't have sex—not our kind of people!" "No!" everyone shouts, and the boat zooms away.

"We're part of their script?" I ask, incredulous. Ilana confirms that she, too, has heard this more than once.

I climb into my tent, whip on my civilian clothes, and run to catch the boat to Mermaid Dock. Still thoughts of wine, but since it's morning I stop instead at an internet café. The ashram has no outbound internet for guests so we have to go to Nassau—which most days, we have no time to do. I order a large latte, then another, a jittery cat mainlining cream.

I get back just in time for brunch and pot washing. Then, after a luxurious nap, I walk from the campground to the ocean by following the fence that separates the ashram from Club Med. Half way there's a massive hole, like someone had shot a cannon through the chain link. How does anyone have the energy to sneak next door to party after *satsang*? We need permission to leave the ashram grounds at night, and lights out is eleven o'clock. It's expressly forbidden to impersonate holiday-makers. "Use of facilities of other hotels without payment is trespassing. Disregard of this rule will result in immediate expulsion from the yoga retreat," our information package stressed.

Clearly, the ashram has a very different vision of paradise than its neighbours—and most people. I continue along the fence, wondering again whether I'm on the wrong side.

At the beach, I sit down to enjoy an orange I've been too busy to eat for days. White sand, blue sky, warm sun, citrus scent, and as usual a perfect eighty degrees. Content, I fold my clothes on my towel and dive into the turquoise, eyes open, a salt-water being returning home. I splash around, light-limbed and giddy, and float for ages, driftwood in the waves. Then a powerboat roars up and parks beside me. Two women get out, and the engine idles as they flirt with the men on board. *Strange place for an ashram*, I'm thinking, as I walk back out of the sea.

I nap on the beach a while, then decide it's time for more chocolate kisses. "Who would open an ashram here?" I ask Mahadevi. She tells me that when Swami Vishnu first came to Paradise Island, it had been serene. He'd received a ninety-nine-year lease on the property from a grateful, wealthy woman whose heroin-addicted child he'd helped.

Swami Vishnu had applied the Five Points of Yoga, part of what we're learning as teacher trainees, she says. These, based on the instructions of his guru, Swami Sivananda, are Proper Exercise, Proper Breathing, Proper Relaxation, Proper Diet, Positive Thinking (Meditation). Nowadays,

Mahadevi adds, developers are hungry for the ashram's property. They want it to relocate, and have even offered a private island.

"So why don't they move?" I ask, thinking about all the distractions.

"Swami Vishnu has blessed this ashram," she shrugs. Apparently, the spirit of a saint may choose to remain in a place, making it the abode of divine qualities such as peace, bliss, and wisdom.

I stroll in the garden, munching chocolate kisses and wondering how you recognize a saint, an enlightened being. I spot Vishnu, a South American guy who lives and works at the ashram on a karma yoga study program. He's up a ladder making repairs.

"Vishnu, I have to ask you something," I call.

He descends the ladder and smiles.

"How do you recognize a saint?"

"I don't know. But I heard that making a hole in your head is a shortcut to enlightenment," he says. He switches on the power drill. "Interested?" he asks, lunging after me.

After the levity of our day "off," it's back to the hard temple floor and discipline for week two. It's hard to imagine that for nearly four decades, students, staff, and guests have gathered twice daily here to meditate, chant, and receive spiritual guidance during *satsang*. Attendance is required, I'd read in my course materials, because "any other activity at these times diminishes the energy of this sacred place."

That morning at breakfast, I hear that some teacher trainees have already fled. Presumably they've realized this is not a relaxed place to do yoga and eat vegetarian food, but a yoga boot camp. The novelty of week one is past, and I feel rebellion at the strict schedule and rules, especially the way they take attendance what seems like every five minutes. I remind myself that it's February, and of my sister's email report that it was so cold at home she had to plug her car in. Time, perhaps, to read the "mind balks at discipline" section of my training manual. Do they push our buttons on purpose, or is it just the best way to control seventy students, to make sure we don't wander off, and perhaps even learn something?

Our teacher had said that the course was overwhelming by design. "Part of what you have to do to change is give up, let go so something new can enter." He'd warned that the philosophy class would make people especially insane, with hundreds of terms they'd never heard before. His advice was to sit still in meditation "for the gift of seeing who you are in silence," and regarding chanting, to "let go and sing."

Luckily, I find our lessons intriguing. Now we're talking about the eight-limb path of yoga, "an ancient science of living in harmony with yourself and others." Doing yoga and *pranayama* four hours a day agrees with me. My body is stronger, my breathing is freer, and I feel harmonious, ready for anything.

I also feel like a leaky pot. My head brims with new yogic ideas and Sanskrit terms. Plus there's anatomy, about which I know little. Our anatomy teacher is animated and knowledgeable. He describes yoga as "a magnificent set of potent techniques to acquire health." I feel a surge of excitement when he adds, "the *asanas* put coherency into a life that's chaotic."

As the week goes on, I notice that the counsellors, who sit at picnic tables at designated hours, are getting busy. People cry, want to drop out, get sick and upset. We're still struggling to get used to the schedule. We only have about two hours a day free in which to do homework, eat, shower, and do laundry. The latter is becoming a real flashpoint. There are only two machines, so it's a fight to keep our two uniforms clean. As an added challenge, the shop, which sells tokens and soap, isn't open at the same time as the laundry room.

Then the rain begins. It lasts three days. One man has a complete meltdown and insists he *must* do his laundry. He's screaming and yelling, quite irrational. People feel sorry at his distress. Two guests, yoga-teacher-trainee graduates, kindly put his clothes in the dryer while we're in class.

On retreat, it's noticeable how small things become big. Your mind grasps at dramas, fights going inward. The usual distractions are gone, so it tries to manufacture new ones. The yogis call it "monkey mind." The rare times I can focus on my breath for any length of time, I see how disorderly and agitating my thoughts actually are. When I tell Polly this, she says in the tone of an expert, "Staying distracted is way easier than being quiet." It's a hedge against emptiness, she adds, and prevents uncomfortable questions such as, "What am I doing here?"

and "What is the meaning of life?"

Ilana, who has now been given a wooden doorstep to prevent campground mud from getting in her tent, has decided we're reincarnated sisters. We've also formed a laundry alliance. Unfortunately, we'd decided hand-washing was the way to go, so our second uniforms remain soaked on the line as the rain continues. We get more disreputable and filthy each day.

My tent fills with water where the mattress touches the wall. One woman who is camping near bathrooms says the smell of the sewer is strong. I wince, but she says it's okay, she's immune, as she works in a microbiology lab. As the swami has been saying: our reactions are dictated by conditioning versus some objective "reality."

Back in the temple that evening, the air is redolent of tiger balm. Everyone is sore after all the hours of sitting in meditation and in lectures, plus four hours of daily yoga. We fidget and shift, trying to find a bearable position. People try to arrive early to get a spot along a wall so they can lean, and many fall asleep, heads on their chests. Energies surge when Gopala leads the chants, inflaming passions with his zealous *kirtan*. I've started playing the tambourine and chanting, but I feel like a fake.

Amid hardships are transcendent moments. At the teacher trainee talent show, an attractive student from California sings "Nature Boy." His sultry voice seeps into the humid twilight. "The greatest thing you'll ever learn, is just to love, and be loved in return." These words, sung in this place devoted to love and kindness and peace, move me. His melody, blessedly, replaces my inner Tony Bennett—"I saw your face, and I ascended"—sound-loop.

Another perfect moment comes at dawn on the morning that the weather finally clears. We walk in silence down the dark beach and sit on the sand in meditation to wait for sunrise. How many sunrises will I see in my life? I wonder, and feel sad—and then wonder if that thought is sophomoric. As the sky grows golden I feel open to some benign grace and chant with an open heart and no sense of irony.

I tell Polly I feel there's something valuable going on here. She laughs as if that's evident and I'm a slow learner. "I'll bet you were a temple sweeper in a past life," she says. "Yeah, in the temple day after day, and finally one day you thought, 'There's something in this.' And then poof, you were gone!"

We imagine my reincarnations: birth after birth, the person who glimpses wisdom while standing on the threshold of death, and then disappears into the next realm. Strangely plausible, I find.

Pot scrubbing ends early one day, so I stop at the shop to visit Mahadevi before the noon lecture. "How it's going?" she asks.

"Everyone is exhausted," I tell her. "The schedule is nuts."

"Wait until next week," she says with a knowing smile. "That's when people *really* freak out."

My headache from caffeine withdrawal is finally gone. I buy anise tea and ask about a pendant Polly had purchased. "I think it had something to do with the blue guy," I tell Mahadevi as she shows me the jewellery.

"Krishna," she says.

I pick up some silver feet, but am not certain this is the same necklace I'd admired. "Do you have anything Krishna-related besides feet?"

Mahadevi starts to laugh. I think maybe she hasn't understood, so I add, "You know, like, some other Krishna body part?"

She laughs harder, and weeps. When she recovers enough to wheeze, "No, only Krishna's feet." The line sets off a new explosion of laughter.

"Tell me what's funny," I implore.

"Well, it's kind of like you just asked, 'Do you have anything related to Christ, except not on a cross? Maybe on a star instead?'"

"We're studying the *Gita*—I guess we aren't there yet," I say, feeling foolish.

She tells me the story of Krishna's feet, which I gather symbolize the value of humility. Krishna is one of Vishnu's twenty-two incarnations, sent to earth to fight for good and conquer evil. I love the complex yogic tales—Krishna, for example, the divine herdsman, is a prankster who cheats and steals and makes love to the gopis, the milkmaids. He's inspired volumes of hot poetry to the beloved.

As I check out the jewellery, I recall a passage from Mirabai, a sixteenth-century Indian poet: "The colours of the Dark One have penetrated Mira's body; all the other colours washed out. Making love with the Dark One and eating little, those are my pearls and my carnelians . . . "

I decide on an *Om* necklace, feeling conflicted about how everything becomes a commodity, including this prehistorical sacred symbol of the Hindu trinity. It feels distressingly good to buy something.

In class, we'd been learning about Brahman and the Hindu trinity. Brahman is "the one," the ultimate reality: formless, eternal, and the source of all existence, which has no attributes. Everything with form is a manifestation of this—knowable aspects that come from and go back to Brahman.

The trinity—Brahma, the creator, Vishnu the preserver, and Shiva, the destroyer—are the main manifestations of Brahman. I feel affinity for Vishnu, the preserving force of the world. Fitting, I guess, that I've been drawn here, to the ashram of his namesake. Vishnu symbolizes goodness and compassion. It's said that people involved in creating harmony in the world are drawn to this energy.

The main thing that's ruining my harmony this week is that it's so hard to find time to get to the beach for a swim. One morning I plan like a general. I wear my bathing suit under my uniform for *satsang* and yoga, run and get my brunch and leave it on a beach chair, and dive into the sea. My vision is bad, so it's a fuzzy blue world. *Hey, is that movement near my breakfast?*

I get out to investigate and find seagulls had been eating my peanut butter and jam sandwich, so someone had pulled my yoga mat over top, and now it's covered in sticky crap. I eat what's left of breakfast, run to do my karma yoga, then have no time to change before lecture. For the rest of the day, until after dinner when I can get back to my tent, I'm damp and sandy.

In the temple the evening before our day off, we yoga teacher trainees are ecstatic at the prospect of free time. I listen to "Sweet Home Alabama" and the rest of the cruise boat playlist, while my mind refuses to meditate for a half hour, and then we chant. Instead of a lecture, we watch a film about Swami Vishnu. He's charismatic, dynamic, has a gift for promoting yoga. When the Beatles were in the Bahamas on location, filming their 1965 film *Help!* near the ashram, Swami Vishnu gave each of the Fab Four a signed copy of his *Complete Illustrated Book of Yoga*. Ringo reportedly said something about not even being able to stand on his legs, let alone his head, while George asked intelligent questions. Swami Vishnu is credited with giving George Harrison his first book about yoga, setting off a lifelong fascination with Eastern philosophy.

The footage about his peace missions surprises me. In the 1970s, "the Flying Swami," as he was called by the international press, "bombarded" areas of conflict with marigolds and peace leaflets. He flew in a groovy Piper Apache peace plane painted with stars and *Om* symbols by millionaire artist Peter Max and travelled on a passport he'd made himself. On one mission, he and his friend Peter Sellers went to Belfast. Immigration came to arrest them, but Sellers did his Indian impression. The officials laughed, asked for autographs, and let the two men stay. They sat on the steps of the Irish Parliament cross-legged, chanting and passing out flowers and leaflets.

In 1971, Swami Vishnu was nearly shot down over the Suez Canal, chased by Israeli jets, and then arrested by the Egyptians. In a Cairo prison he was happy because it was quiet and he could meditate. When the authorities realized he wasn't a spy, that he was on a peace mission, he went from prisoner to VIP. His captors fed him dates and insisted on taking him out to his first nightclub—which he found so noisy and smoky he asked to be returned to his cell. He'd liked the women, he said later. They had really good control over their abdominal muscles.

That night as we file out of the temple after *arati*, the trainees are inspired, the plants are happy after the rain, and everything's imbued with a feeling of promise, that this life is precious, and we need to do something useful with our time on earth.

Week three, which we'd been warned is "the toughest week," gets off to a good start. We're back after our heavenly day of freedom—during which most of us loafed and swam and drank coffee and ate illicit foods on the mainland. I've noticed my desire to eat sea creatures has faded. I have no more hungry interludes when I sit in meditation, plotting to feast on yellow-fin tuna grilled with mango salsa, or red snapper, followed by crab and lobster with clarified butter. Now I'm more likely to fantasize about salty kale chips. My desire for wine, however, continues unabated, and I haven't had a drink in oh so long. I pick up an email that's been printed out for me and stuck on the bulletin board. It's from my drinking buddies in Toronto, asking how things are going at the Betty Ford clinic. I laugh, and wish I could transport myself to their kitchen, well into our first bottle of chardonnay and the week's stories.

This morning, we'll be trying *kriyas*, or cleansing practices. We gather on the beach platform and watch as the garden swami shows us how to insert a catheter into our noses, in one side and out the other. Then we each drink eight cups of salt water, after which we're to go to the beach to throw up. Soon, people are vomiting everywhere. I wonder what the people at Club Med and tourists strolling down the beach make of this. I tell our *asana* teacher that nothing is happening. "Oh well, it will come out one end or the other," he says mildly. I go back to the water's edge and stick my fingers down my throat. This time, I succeed.

Next day, the rock-star arrival of Bhagavan Das and his entourage creates a buzz. He was the first western disciple of Neem Karoli Baba. During this time he became a mentor to Ram Dass, who featured him in the classic book, *Be Here Now*. It's nearly Maha Shivaratri, one of the most sacred nights on the yogic calendar, and Bhagavan will lead continuous Shiva chants from dusk until dawn. He is an expert in nada yoga, the path of mystical union through sound.

When this holy night for spiritual purification and rebirth arrives, Bhagavan plays a one-stringed guitar-like instrument and sings, accompanied by tabla drums. He's tall and thin with a piled up hairdo, long beard, and wild eyebrows. His muscled helpers, or bodyguards, look like they might start doing crowd control. Everyone gets into the groove, repeating, "Om Namah Shivaya," evoking the energy of Shiva. It's hypnotic. Polly and I resolve to start leading *kirtan* as it seems like such a great gig. I think fleetingly of home, worlds away from this warmth and colour and music.

As the chants continue, a tantric priest from South India who does arati in the temple, conducts elaborate *pujas*, sacred ceremonies. He offers flowers and incense as homage to Shiva and bathes a *linga*, a phallic-looking stone, in milk and honey. I'm told the night's rituals are symbolic of the union of consciousness and matter—the dance of universal creation—and will end in the marriage of Shiva and Parvati at dawn. If you take part, supposedly you can be freed from past sins, dwell in enlightened bliss, and reach *moksha*, liberation from the cycle of life and death. Predictably, long before the dawn feast, which is a final offering to Shiva made when the sun comes up, I'm fast asleep.

In the days that follow, Bhagavan leads *kirtan* in the temple. Each morning, another lovely young woman sits up front gazing at him rapturously, a fresh hibiscus flower in her hair. "What is he doing to those girls?" Polly whispers, eyebrows raised.

When the basket of musical instruments comes out, I choose a shaker and a drum, diversifying from my usual choice of tambourine. I even start to clap when we get to the part in Jaya Ganesha that goes, "Jaya guru, siva guru, hari guru, raam." Embracing my inner *bhakti* yogi—or just bored? My favourite learning topic this week is the truth of interdependence, how insight about this arises naturally in yoga. This reflects my own experience, though I'd have been hard pressed to explain it to anyone. When you re-link body and mind, when you're at peace, a feeling of unity arises. The swami says one of the reasons we're so out of touch is we don't see that we are all related, all one. Many of our problems—personal, societal, environmental—are because we've forgotten this simple reality.

During our *asana* classes, Polly has been noticing that her tongue keeps doing peculiar things. She goes to ask the swamis about it. I'd seen photos in a book of advanced breathing practices that looked like what she was doing. I thought they'd tell her she'd been a yogi in a past life, or something flakey like that.

"So what did they say?" I ask.

"That I need a psychiatrist," she says with a smirk.

When Bhagavan Das leaves, taking his fame dust with him, things take a downward slide. One of the swamis scolds Gopala publicly, telling him to tone down his chanting. Repressed sexual energy throbs everywhere. The negativity that our teacher foresaw is powerful. People are mainly sick of "discipline and dogma and new-age dipshit," as one man puts it. I see what he means, but I try to steer clear, to focus on what's intriguing and ignore the rest.

By now, seven people from my class have dropped out. An embarrassed British man in his sixties tells me he was kidding himself, this isn't for him, and he's leaving. An American woman in her twenties whispers to everyone who will listen, "This place is *messed up*," and then goes home. A thin, hyper woman with corkscrew hair sobs in her boyfriend's arms because staff asked whether she was on drugs. The son of a scion, who had dropped out the previous week, returns, saying that this experience is changing his life.

Our teachers seem to think everyone needs more discipline; but I'd like more freedom. I feel the teachers suffer from compassion deficit disorder. We all get upset when a young British woman's temperature reaches 104 degrees, and the teachers are reluctant to call a doctor. Her friend uses cold towels to cool the fever and, when it doesn't drop, calls a physician herself. The teachers shrug, say, "It's karma," and act as though she should be grateful to be getting rid of it through her suffering. I think they're cruel and irresponsible.

I catch a cold. Snakes are living near our tents, and everyone is afraid to go for a midnight pee. I start to lose it. One day waiting for yoga class to begin on the bay platform, I wave at the boats and yell, "Save us, it's a cult!" Soon, other yellow-and-white-clad students line up and wave too, and people on the boats wave back. The tourist boat slows, and we hear the familiar refrain. "This here's the yoga ash-ram..."

The evening before our day off, I'm desperate for some time alone. I plan a *satsang* escape. Outside the temple on the way in, I place my shoes strategically. During silent meditation, as "Sweet Home Alabama" begins and all eyes are closed, I roll backwards over the low wall at the back of the temple. I evade all swamis despite my telltale yellow and whites, and slip undetected into a hammock by the sea. Wind blows, waves crash, palms sway, and I soak up my incomparable stolen pleasure—solitude.

Week four flies by, and we start missing everything before we've even left.

I feel affection for the green, well-tended grounds; the signs with messages like *Unity in Diversity*; the endearing traits of our teachers, who last week I thought were mean and petty; and even my tent. I can't believe I've slept there for nearly a month. I have no memory of being inside it, as

I'm always exhausted, then unconscious. After pot washing one morning, my boss from the kitchen invites me to join him in Val Morin to do karma yoga in the summer. I can't believe that actually sounds like a good idea.

A month feels like a long time to spend here. Most of us grumbled and even despaired, but now we say we wouldn't have missed it. It's as though we've integrated what they were trying to teach us. We know what a yoga lifestyle is, how the ashram is conducive to it, and what the benefits are. I feel strong, centred, purposeful.

As I go about the daily schedule, my mind strays home. I can't wait to see Antonio. But when I recall the usual rush and routine of my working life, I feel utterly bored. Modern-day tedium. This place may not be perfect, but the yogic teachings make sense to me, and it's never, ever humdrum.

One afternoon, our orange-robed teacher sits up on his dais, while behind him on the bay, pleasure boats form a moving tableau. We sit cross-legged on the hard floor or on our yoga mats, fidgeting less than before. He's delivering a lecture about the nature of reality. We all want the same thing, he says—some call it happiness, others, peace. We run after worldly pleasures because we're seeking happiness, not the objects themselves. These things are fleeting, which is why we are perpetually looking for something more.

As he talks, the massive hull of a cruise ship called *Illusion* glides up, coasts behind him and emerges on his other side. In a flash, this place, these teachings, all make sense. This isn't the wrong place for a yoga school. It's ideal. The fleeting pleasures the swami is talking about, Nassau's "good life," constantly break in. Paradise Island ashram: a nature-of-reality show.

The swami continues, accompanied by sirens across the bay and vibrations from the ground when planes take off on water. Finally, I hear about the difference between good and pleasant, as Omkara the *bramacharya* had promised me at breakfast on my first day. You need a healthy body in order to do spiritual practice, the swami explains, which is why we do yoga postures. You need a healthy mind in order to do spiritual practice, which is why we meditate. And *viveka*, ultimate discrimination, he says, is the fruit of long yoga and meditation practice.

"*Viveka*," the swami continues, "is the faculty that discriminates the real from the unreal, the permanent from the fleeting, the good from the pleasant."

The "pleasant" relates to the path of ignorance, of sensual pleasures that don't last, he says. This path doesn't lead anywhere. The "good" is the path of wisdom, which is not always easy, but that leads to freedom.

I like that there's no concept of sin attached to sensual pleasure; it's just that you won't grow by clinging to what's fleeting. But I still can't decide whether my bread was good, or pleasant. Can't something be both?

Toward the end of the week, we study for our exam, held the Saturday morning before the course ends. I'm surprised by how much I've learned, mainly experiential knowledge, recorded in my body and my cells. As for the onslaught of the *Bhagavad Gita*, yoga philosophy, and anatomy—for those subjects it's been a crash course, but I have good books and notes for future reference. I can see how all this will sustain me as I begin to teach.

The swamis tell us that what we've received are seeds. We may not understand at first but when we practice and gain experience, they will sprout. They reiterate that we should never accept anything we can prove to ourselves by our own experiments. Just follow the ancient yogic map and see for yourself, they say. There's no need to seek freedom in distant lands: it exists within, in our own bodies, hearts, minds, and spirits. Inner space offers realms as vast as external geographies to explore.

Saturday arrives. During the exam, Ilana and I are annoyed to learn we only needed to know the first stanza of the *Gajananam*. Our group photo is taken on the beach platform: the swamis in orange in the centre, amid a sea of yellow and white. Ilana sits in front holding Swami Sivananda's photo, while another student holds Swami Vishnu's. Polly and I, like the kids in the hall we once were, lurk at the back, with Mahadevi. Polly sees the photo later and says, "I look like a crack whore." I laugh so hard I fall off the path and into some ferns.

That evening, at our final *satsang*, "Sweet Home Alabama" and silent meditation become one. Eyes open as usual, I look around, thinking back to our teacher/counsellor's advice from the first week. Be open, try things, judge for yourself.

As the harmonium gives its breathy wheeze, and I begin singing and clapping with the others; I find the whole thing energizing and joyous. Then Gopala chants, electrifying us all, uncensored by the teachers. I feel—well, mortified, actually—to realize that I'm quite a devotional person. My self-concept isn't elastic enough to go from cringing through the *hari krishnas* the first week to acknowledging this openly, not just yet. Why are the best discoveries in my life made when I allow myself be led by a mysterious impulse, despite what my rational mind says?

The swamis wish us well, and as the priest waves the flames for the last *arati*, I feel a pang, wondering whether this ritual to remove darkness will soon be replaced by TV after supper on wintry Ontario nights. I've often been irritated, skeptical, and exhausted here, but the flickering ghee-wick candles and the haunting melody of this ancient ritual haven't failed to enchant and console me. We accept *prasad* and find our shoes, all urgency gone. Newly minted yoga teachers gather at the Health Hut to say goodbyes over anise tea. We chat into the night, our last one in yellow and whites. We joke about how life will be without pyjamas and vow to keep in touch. Mahadevi predicts that many of us will be back. I say I hope she's right, wish her goodnight, and wander happily off to bed.

Next morning, Ilana and I hug on the dock as she waits for the boat. She's dressed in skinny jeans, a glitter shirt, and her clunky shoes. It's weird to see her regain this identity. The tourist boat slows down and a megaphone man starts his usual spiel. We laugh and cry and chant, "Om Trayambakam," a mantra to guarantee her a safe and auspicious journey. And we promise that whenever we do our laundry, we'll smile and think of one another.

Polly and I stay on. We walk down the beach to coral-pink monstrosity, Atlantis, to see the aquariums. The place boasts "the largest man-made marine habitat with eleven exhibit lagoons, home to more than fifty thousand sea animals." It also has the biggest casino in the Caribbean, bars, lounges, waterfalls, pools, and a faux Mayan temple with waterslides. It's tacky as hell, quite a shock. As we cut through a courtyard being prepared for an event, Polly grabs a bottle of wine and stuffs it into her knapsack. We walk back down the beach, to the quieter end past the ashram, and sit on the sand. We open the bottle and pour wine into cups we've scavenged.

"To Vishnu, the preserver," I say. Polly and I click plastic cups and drink. The wine tastes pleasant, but not as good as I'd been imagining.

We talk a while about life after Jaya Ganesha and six hours a day sitting on hard temple floors and "silent" meditation accompanied by Lynyrd Skynyrd. What will endure like the mud stains on our white pants? What will fade like our tans once we leave Paradise Island? Despite our compromising behaviour, we agree that we feel changed. For one thing, the yoga teacher training course taught us new, if intermittent, self-control. And while we both came to learn to teach postures, that's the least of what we're taking away.

Here, now, tipsy and feeling at one with the sand under my feet, the twinkling stars above, inhaling and exhaling to the tidal rhythm of waves that sound like breath, I tell Polly I'm happy to have found something I respect: imperfect, easy to mock, but with goals I support wholeheartedly. Feeling messianic, I say I am a propagator of yoga, part of an ancient tradition for peace, that of Vishnu the preserver.

I'm also an undisciplined fool, I decide as Polly refills our cups—but tonight, under the boundless sky, no longer a complete stranger in paradise.

Saint's Embrace

THE SWEET, GAP-TOOTHED SMILE OF AMMA BEAMS DOWN FROM stickers plastered all over the interior of our speeding autorickshaw. Her plump face whips by on posters and billboards as we bump along the road to Vallikavu, a tiny coastal backwater town in south India.

The driver swoops like a swallow and rolls to a halt at the foot of a gleaming white bridge. It arcs across a wide canal, to where a bubblegum pink city rises out of the green coconut palms. "The pot of gold at the end of the rainbow," I groan irritably.

We've arrived at the school of Sri Amritanandamayi Devi—Amma for short—Kerala's "Hugging Saint." I don't want to be here, but my companions insisted. Part rock star and part spiritual leader, Amma, a round woman in a white sari, spreads her message of unconditional love in spectacular hug-a-thons around the world. Despite myself, I find her intriguing. Why does she give hugs? Why do people want them?

One of India's few female gurus, she's revered as an incarnation of the Divine Mother. But she's also a rebel who seems to have broken all India's taboos at once. This "mother of absolute bliss," as her name translates, hugs people of all sexes and castes—an inflammatory act for south India. Also, the scraps of her story I've heard are winningly weird: born blue and cross-legged, heals lepers by sucking pus, tames snakes, and survived various murder attempts.

I sigh, heave my carry-on-size Samsonite up the many steps of the bridge. Stairs, the absence of pavement, red betel-nut spit—just three of India's many unforeseens. Antonio and our friends Sue and Melanie walk on, knapsacks on their backs, steps light, as I bump my suitcase up, then down the other side. I wheel and drag it through red sand, past an Ayurvedic health centre, a tall pink high rise, and a few smaller ones, until I reach the main temple. Atop it, Arjuna and Krishna, straight out of the *Bhagavad Gita*, ride into karmic battle in their ornate chariot.

Up about a hundred more stairs is the International Office, where I catch up to my friends. A young American at the front desk finds us a room for four: 150 rupees each per night, or not quite four dollars Canadian, including basic meals. I'm pleasantly surprised that the ashramites have no issue with Antonio and three women sharing quarters.

Right now, the ashram is abuzz, the American explains, because Amma, who is on the road half the year, is home giving blessings. About 3,000 full-time residents live here, he tells us: mainly Amma's monastic students, who include about 300 Westerners, and now, thousands of visitors have flooded in.

The air is charged with excitement, and people all around us are engaged in purposeful activity. The entire ashram is run by volunteers, the American adds, waving around us toward the travel office, shop, second-hand store, and publications office, all housed in this building.

Back down the stairs and across the temple square, we pick up standard-issue pillows and blankets then cram into a high-rise elevator to our room. The doors close to reveal more Amma stickers—Amma looking impish, Amma in front of a waterfall. We stare at them until we reach the ninth floor of the fifteen-storey tower.

Our room is incredibly clean and spacious. We hear the slapping of clothes being washed, *bhajans* blasting through a loudspeaker, and the ubiquitous cawing of Indian crows.

First stop in our explorations is the "Western canteen." A polished volunteer in her fifties takes my order of coffee and peanut butter and toast. "I told Amma I didn't want to be in the spotlight as that's where I've been all my life," the woman says in a French accent. The comment seems apropos of nothing. "And this is where she puts me," she continues with an affectionate laugh. "Front and centre again."

A sign on the wall warns us to protect our food from crows, and from the resident Pallas fishing eagle. "I've seen it swoop right down and take off with someone's omelette," a woman who is wiping down tables tells us.

An extremely shaky volunteer has been put in charge of clean dishes, and they rattle unnervingly as he walks past. "Amma obviously has a sense of humour," Antonio whispers, and we all laugh. It's pleasant to watch as people of all ages, from all walks of life—Indian and Western, mainly dressed in the white of devotees, many with young children in tow—rush past.

We don't realize until it's too late that everyone is making haste to the temple, where Amma is presiding. The doors are closed by the time we get there, and we're unsure about trying to slip in. So instead we walk to the beach and watch the molten gold of the Arabian Sea as the sun goes down. To sit quietly by the water is a relief after our bone-jarring trip from Cochin on an ancient bus and the ashram's dizzying activity and music.

Local men sitting near us on the rocks tell us about the tsunami, which took 140 lives on this beach. Amma rebuilt the houses and constructed the huge bridge we'd crossed earlier to ensure quick evacuation if a tsunami ever happened again. The ashram, they add—which is located between the sea and the canal that extends far along the coast—was the centre of relief operations.

When we return to the pink city after dark it's still deserted. We sit on the temple steps, where we mock a publication we find there. It's like Oprah's magazine, except with Amma on the front. Inside are photos taken after the tsunami: ashramites in waist-deep water leading villagers to safety and evacuating the hospital, and providing free food and shelter for hundreds of homeless. And there's the opening of the bridge, which Amma built to connect the seaside peninsula and the ashram to mainland Kerala.

We'd been making jokes, but as we turn the pages, the scale and scope of Amma's humanitarian activities impress us: aid for victims of Hurricane Katrina, among many disaster relief programs; orphanages; and suicide prevention programs for Kerala's farmers, who, due to crop losses and rising debt, often died horrific deaths from drinking pesticides in desperation.

Other programs supplied free food, medicine, pensions, and houses for the poor; free legal aid; homes for the elderly; programs to empower women; educational institutes, including a university; hospitals, apparently among the best-equipped in south India; and an Ayurvedic health institute. Amma's nongovernmental organization, linked to the United Nations, has a global network of charitable projects.

We leave the magazine on the steps and wander around the grounds. A small house built into a larger structure, with a tiny temple next to it, attracts us. This is the original house where Amma grew up, and the temple is the cowshed where she first started giving hugs.

The story goes that she would lead the cows and goats out, then bring people in and console them. Now, *pujas*, ceremonies, are held here, and the inner sanctum features a photo of Amma surrounded by flower offerings. These days, when she's not travelling, the saint lives in two small rooms nearby.

It's obvious *satsang* is over when people come swarming out of the temple around eight o'clock. Everything opens back up. I buy an Amma watch for 200 rupees, a CD of *bhajans*, and have a strawberry milkshake at the juice bar—which has separate pickup windows for "ladies" and "gents."

I also buy some soap with Amma's face on the package, made here at her Ayurvedic institute, and two of her many biographies. Thirty books of Amma's teachings and life story, plus scriptural commentary, songs, poetry, and Sanskrit mantras are available in the shop or online—in twenty-five languages. Amma, I learn from a devotee selling *malas*, prayer beads, has large centres in Australia, Belgium, France, Germany, Japan, Singapore, and the United States.

On the temple steps across from juice bar, we sit down to people watch. I end up engrossed in my Amma books. I read that she was born in 1957, cross-legged and blue, just like Krishna and Divine Mother Kali, two deities she later embodied.

She suffered as a child. Her parents, fisherfolk, were prejudiced because she had darker skin—it turned in time from blue to dark brown. She was forced to leave school and serve the family, cooking and cleaning like a slave. When her divine calling started to manifest, her parents thought she was crazy. She went into trances, danced blissfully at the seashore and sang holy songs. She also gave away the family's food to the hungry and brought the homeless to live in their cowshed—for which she was beaten.

Worse, Amma—then still called by the name her parents had given her, Sudhamani, "Ambrosial Jewel"—broke dangerous taboos. A fourteen-year-old girl would be strictly prohibited from touching men. By this age, she hugged everyone, irrespective of sex or caste.

I had an inkling of how serious this disregard for conventions could be. Here in Kerala, at a restaurant where we ate regularly, Antonio had once reached out to touch the sleeve of the woman serving food, to get her attention. Her husband, usually so friendly, had run over and banged his hand hard on the table. "No!" he yelled in fury. We were shocked.

Amma's brother, the book continued, was tired of how she dishonoured the family by hugging men, and tried to kill her with a knife. She had many enemies within her own family, among the villagers, and from the Committee to Stop Blind Beliefs, a "rationalist group" that harassed and beat her. She had survived several attempts on her life.

Early on, Amma had seen the world as being pervaded with the energy of Krishna, my other book said. Later she saw the energy of the Devi, the Divine Mother, in everything. That's when she became the incarnation of the Devi, the embodiment of pure love.

But few had believed that this unschooled little fisher-girl was a God-realized being. There's a saying in the local language, Malayalam, "The jasmine that grows in the front of the house has no fragrance"—which is to say the person who becomes great won't be recognized in his or her own community, the book explained.

Eventually, Amma's miracles won everyone over. In the "Miracle of the Pudding" she made water into milk, and then into *panchamritam*, a dessert of milk, bananas, and raw sugar. Even after 1,000 people ate the pudding, the story goes, the bowl remained full. After this miracle, the villagers finally accepted her divinity.

I skimmed through many other tales. The leper story of how she healed a man named Dattan by sucking pus and spitting it in a bowl again and again. How she survived a run-in with a deadly cobra that terrorized the village. The snake had slithered into Amma's cowshed/temple, and while everyone ran in fear, Amma grabbed the snake and touched her tongue to its tongue. "This is my grandmother," Amma said. "Don't hurt her."

Animals were drawn to Amma, just like her followers. In May 1981, when she was twenty-four, the tiny temple and the white-painted family house we'd seen earlier on the grounds was designated as an ashram.

I close the Amma books when someone strolls nonchalantly past with an elephant. I'm surprised how few Western devotees look like new-agey, hippie types. Many seem to be young couples with kids, or over-fifties. One devotee who sits nearby, enjoying the starry night, tells me she left a successful marketing career in Vancouver to join Amma and serve others. "I'm planning to die here," she tells me with a smile. There are many other professionals like her at the ashram, she confirms, all tired of doing only for themselves. She adds that life here is very intense, not a bit like retirement.

The woman encourages us to go and get a token that will let us join the hug queue for the following day. Amma will be giving *darshan*, or blessings. My ill-humour has abated and I'm eager to see this. What will the worshipped God-as-mother, or the feminine principle, *shakti*, look like?

Ashram days begin at four forty-five in the temple, when a swami leads the recitation of the 108 names of Amma in Sanskrit, followed by the 1001 names of the Supreme Mother. I don't make it, waking up just in time to have breakfast and get to the great hall for eleven o'clock, when the blessings begin.

Thousands of people sit in chairs waiting. Many more crowd the aisles. At the front, white-robed monks and nuns chant, and the room vibrates with music: the harmonium, tabla drums, clapping. Amma's divine musicians, some dressed in the orange of Hindu swamis, sing and play, a starring attraction in their own right.

The music swells as Amma takes the stage. A plump, barefoot woman in a white cotton sari, she raises her arms as though holding a large ball and dances a little. "She's calling down the Divine Goddess," a white-clad woman tells me. Amma soon disappears from view, sitting on a low cushion at the centre of her hive of devotees, ready to spread her message of unconditional love.

The organizers tell us to return around one thirty when our numbers are likely to be coming up. Three lines form—one for men, one for women, and one for Westerners and others who have travelled a long way to be here. All converge on the saint. It's pandemonium. I don't see how Amma can possibly hug the thousands of pilgrims.

Apparently, she just keeps going, sometimes all night. Why does she give hugs? I ask another woman in white.

"The BBC asked her that once. She said, 'Why does a river flow? It's my nature.'"

Outside the hall, I turn to my companions. "Why do you want a hug anyway?"

Antonio shrugs, "Maybe it will help something."

"I want to have contact with a woman I believe is pure, like the momma I never had," Melanie says. "Only good can come from it," Sue adds. As for me, I find Amma interesting—but what can a hug really change?

When we return at one thirty as instructed, we're directed into a long line, where we stand for a half hour. Then we sit on rows of chairs stage right and move forward row by row, getting ever closer to Amma. From here we can see her smooth face, radiant smile, the flash of a diamond nose ring, her dark hair pulled back in a long plait. She's fifty-seven, but looks twenty years younger.

She has garlands of flowers around her neck, and is in passionate motion. There's something boundless, oceanic about her. I'm struck by how focused she is, at the energy required to do what she's doing. She never charges for her blessings, never turns anyone away, and has hugged about twenty-six million people worldwide in the past thirty-six years.

"She's amazing. So far the longest she's gone is twenty-three hours non-stop," another white-clad devotee whispers.

I guess I expected someone dispensing dry little hugs, not this dynamism, and emotion. I love her joyous gestures, especially when marigolds being heaped around her neck threaten to cover her face.

She places her hands in prayer pose, palms together, fingertips under the garlands. She bows her head, and then suddenly, theatrically, flings up her arms, sending the flowers flying high into the air, where her devotees catch them. The moment feels suspended in time.

The faces of the people who come toward her are mostly full of love and hope, while others are crying. The adoration of her devotees moves me, as does the simplicity of her message. "My religion is love," she proclaims on one of the ubiquitous posters. Amma fervently embraces a wizened old man who lies in her lap. She whispers something in his ear. He looks ecstatic. She grins and unwraps his offering of sweet rice in a banana leaf. The man weeps with joy.

Eventually, we make our way up to stand in the final-approach line. "I'm going to ask her for a mantra for a good husband," Sue jokes with the volunteer, who looks horrified. "Don't do that—she'll give you a lecture on what a mantra is for."

Another volunteer collects our hair clips and glasses and anything else that might poke the saint. We're asked to wipe the sweat from our brows, and as the line moves forward, I'm pushed onto my knees, inserted into the crush. I feel yet another volunteer move my legs and feet into position.

Myopic without my glasses, all I can see is Amma. Her face is round as the full moon, and her brown eyes look warm and mellow. She's hugging someone, saying what sounds like, "Kumari kumari kumari." She is given a banana leaf package that she opens with pleasure. She eats a bit of the sweet inside, and when a volunteer goes to take it, playfully snatches it back, and passes it around to her devotees. The saint's *prasad*, blessed food.

An almighty shove and suddenly, I'm in the arms of Amma. I'd wanted to look into her eyes, but it's too late, so I decide to give her a good squeeze instead. She's rocking me in her sandalwood embrace, saying what I think is "my darling my darling my darling."

She presses a sweet and a packet of sacred ash into my hand. I try to get up and am pushed forward again—this time with Antonio beside me for a three-way hug. Amma pulls us back again and again for another clasp. Finally, she releases us and smiles warmly. Someone gives my glasses back, and we're whisked away to sit on a platform beside the saint.

Here, I feel a particular calm and quiet, like when good friends leave after a visit and I sit down with a cup of tea, thinking loving thoughts. I glance over at Sue. Usually such a hard-ass, she has tears rolling down her cheeks. I turn back to watch Amma. Some people are weeping, others look ecstatic, some appear desperate, or ill. The beauty of her blessing, and of this hunger to receive it. "To lovingly caress people, to console and wipe their tears until the end of this mortal frame—this is Amma's wish."

A woman in white signals that it's time for us to go, for others to take our spot. Once we're outside, Sue says she wants a personal meditation mantra from the saint, so she has to go back when the hugging ends. Impatient as ever, she asks the nearest person who looks like he might know what time that is likely to be. She accosts him repeatedly, oblivious to the huge "In Silence" sign that hangs around his neck.

Antonio and I both seek a quiet spot to consider our Amma experience. This proves difficult. He heads for the high-rise rooftop to meditate amid the blowing laundry, and I opt for the cool, dark temple. Inside, ankle bracelets tinkle amid engine sounds, music, and voices of kids at play and mothers chatting.

The altar is decorated with more images of Amma, one in the style of an Indian deity in front of green rice paddy and coconut trees. I gaze at her and wonder how you recognize a saint. In Hinduism, I'd heard, it isn't like in Catholicism, say, where the Church gives saints a seal of approval. It's based on your intuition, on the experience of peace you feel in the enlightened person's presence. It's said a saint can transmit a seed of wisdom that can later grow.

I slip into the inner sanctum, where people are prostrating. It's a shrine to the wrathful, blue-black goddess Kali, who wears a necklace of severed heads to represent false consciousness, her face and breasts smeared with the blood. Exhausted by all the intensity, I find a quiet corner and gaze into a candle flame, glowing like gold in the dark. But before I can note any effects from the saintly hug, I drift right off to sleep.

Later, after a veggie burger and fries at the Western canteen—after months of veggie *thali*, such bliss—I walk by the great hall. I do this again before bed. Both times, the place is packed, the devotional music still playing, and Amma is hugging her way indefatigably through the snaking lines. Does she ever take breaks—for water, to pee, just to stretch? I ask a devotee. No, he says, and she sleeps just an hour a night. After the hug-a-thon, she has mail to answer and decisions to make about her charitable projects.

I don't make it to the temple at four forty-five the next day either. After breakfast, Sue describes her previous night's mantra experience. Amma had written the mantra's words on a paper, tossed rose petals over Sue, and devotees had bathed her feet in oil, honey, and milk. Then, after nearly sixteen hours of non-stop blessings, Amma had stood up and sashayed down the ramp, palms out to touch those of the followers waiting on both sides. "She is *so cool*," Sue enthuses, kissing her kitschy Amma ring.

I agree—and yet I feel ready to leave. Antonio noted that with the non-stop bhajans blasting through loudspeakers, Amma's ubiquitous face, the emotional hug-a-thons, and chanting the name of the Divine Mother, you have to either leave or start dressing in devotee-whites by the third day.

Amma is giving *darshan* again today, and the air is electric. As we wait for the elevator, four Pallas fishing eagles soar up, held aloft in the currents. I take a last look out at the sea, the stretch of coconut palms bordering the blue canal, and below, at Amma's teeming pink city. When the elevator doors close, I grin back at the stickers of her sweetly smiling face.

Back on the ground floor, I drag my Samsonite through the sand to return my pillow and blankets. The volunteer at the desk tells us that Amma had gone on until two thirty in the morning. I lug my bag toward the bridge, recalling how frequently in India I've had temple priests bow to me, then open their palms to reveal a folded 100-rupee note they're hoping I'll match. Here at Amma's, there's a lot to buy, but not once have I been asked for money.

As I bump my bag up and down the far-side steps and roll though more betel-nut spit, I notice a feeling. There's a lightness in my heart, or a candle-glow—or maybe it's just relief to be on my way? We clamber into an autorickshaw. As it speeds away, Amma's manifold images whip past, and the feeling just keeps on humming, like bees deep in the hive.

Thalaserry Bus

AS SOON AS WE ARRIVE IN THE GREEN HILLS OF MADIKERI, I FEEL
bleak. Antonio chose this place. "It's at the end of the line. It seems like a
good, natural place to go," he'd reasoned. This should have registered as
a warning. I'm wary of his Don Quixote tendencies, of how he would go
"on his way, letting his horse take whatever path it chose, for he believed
that therein lay the very essence of adventures."

This time, enticed by the prospect of splendid tea and Coorg
mountain honey, the aroma of cardamom and black pepper, the
holy river Cauvery, ridge after ridge of slopes laden with forests, I'd
agreed readily. "This god-gifted, pollution-free, calm and quiet land
of mountains cordially invites you to experience its hospitality," read
the Karnataka website, "and make this holiday of yours an interesting
chapter in your life."

Now, descending into bus station bedlam after our 120-kilometre ride
from Mysore, I recall another description of Madikeri: "District headquarter
is standing at the height of about 1,525 metres elevation in the rich green
trap of the Western Ghats."

I look around. It is a green trap. The town appears as though it's
washed down the mountain valley in a rainstorm to the lowest point,
where it's now decaying.

Antonio looks around. "Nice," he says, gesturing at the lush landscape.
"So green." Madikeri was once a hill station where the British went to

escape the heat, he tells me. "The Scotland of India," he adds, "known for its fresh air, hikes, and attractions such as a scenic hilltop where ancient kings had watched the sun set."

Our hotel is dispiriting: tidy and quiet, with a clean, air-conditioned restaurant. Confining. Antonio quite likes it. After a cold night in our cold hotel, we go exploring. In the searing February heat, we walk over a hump-backed bridge on the way to see Madikeri's fort. I wipe away sweat that pours down my face and neck. It gets hotter and hotter here until even the sky can't stand it, I think with annoyance, and the monsoon rains finally burst in protest.

I'm sweltering and peevish. I've also injured my foot. I may be getting the flu. At the apex of the bridge lies a filthy man with no arms or legs. *How did he get here? Who is looking out for him?* I wonder irritably as I trudge on.

The Great Madikeri Fort is not great. Now a government office, it also houses a bare, dusty museum. From the fort, high on a hill, we look down into a prison courtyard. Men sit and talk and mend their sandals, or smoke, or wash their clothes. Also stuck here, I think in solidarity.

Antonio leads me around the fort's ramparts in the blazing heat. He's Brazilian, and there's no climate he loves more. We linger under a tree with huge orange blossoms. I agree, grudgingly and only when he insists, that they're perfection itself.

In the afternoon, we walk seven kilometres through town and into the countryside to a famous waterfall. It's a tedious trickle. The tourism site should have read: *Green tourist trap.*

On our long walk back from the waterfall, Antonio talks about India and expectations. "This country always confounds us," he says.

It's true—in three months in India, it's been by accident that we've experienced transcendent moments, the ones all travellers seek, when you feel the boundaries of your self expand. And on the flip side, every time we heard that a place or event was fantastic, it turned out that it likely had been—once.

In the first category, unforgettable, I choose a day in the countryside when I'd been out for a stroll. Crossing the canal bridge, I'd followed a path between the green tapioca fields and ambled down a lane where children ran out to call, "What's your good name?" and "Howareyoulamfine!" and "Ta-ta." As I turned onto the paved road, an autorickshaw rounded the bend. These three-wheeler taxis look like weird bees, painted yellow and black, with two-stroke engines that buzz as they accelerate. Someone with white hair leaned out from the backseat. As it got closer I realized it was a goat speeding toward me, wind in its face.

The autorickshaw veered over and stopped. The goat's yellow-slit eyes looked at me gravely. A slim, brown, bangled hand emerged from the far side of the backseat. In its palm rested a perfect orange. I squinted into the shaded interior and saw a gorgeous woman in a red silk sari, smiling that warm Kerala smile that makes your heart glow.

She motioned for me to take the bright orange. I took it, cupped my palms around it, bowed and said, "Namaste." The driver hit the gas, the autorickshaw hurtled away, and the blond goat looked back. A deity visitation? A dream? I stood there, staring at the fruit.

As for underwhelming experiences, Antonio and I discuss the possible choices as we kick clods of earth and stones along the dusty Madikeri road. We settle on the day at the Theosophy Society in Chennai, in Tamil Nadu state. We'd been enchanted by the idea of seeing the legendary tree under which Krishnamurti gave his early teachings.

Beyond the nondescript front gates, green parkland threaded with walking trails had beckoned, a refuge amid the concrete and chaos of Chennai. We wandered down shady paths, and I delighted in the coolness. Then we saw a sign: "To the Big Ban Yan"—and a white arrow painted on the ground.

Near the tree many people lingered, some on a stone bench in front of the tree, looking soulful, getting their photos taken. Others, like us, kept a polite distance and sat by a fountain across from the tree, taking a longer view. A young Indian couple smiled at us shyly. I said hello. They were eager to talk. He handed me his card, which said he was a Christian teacher. We all gazed at the tree. Its branches snaked out and spread wide, so wide they were propped up with metal poles.

As I looked at the tree, I noticed something. It was hard to spot at first, because of the grey vines hanging off the serpentine branches. Everything was so intertwined that it created a screen.

I squinted. "Where is the actual tree?" I said.

"What do you mean?" the Indian man said.

"The tree—its trunk. Where is it?"

We all looked. "Oh," he said, and shrugged as though at something of no consequence. "It decayed and had to be removed, I think about four years ago."

I nodded. The banyan was reputed to be 450 years old. Decrepitude was a given. It somehow seemed impolite to mention to the others that there was actually no tree, just braced branches. Finally, the bench in front of Krishnamurti's tree was vacant. The Indian man snapped a few shots of his partner with the tree, and then I took a portrait of Antonio, and he of me.

When we left, people were still gazing, rapt, perhaps inhaling some whiff of ancient wisdom that escaped us at the Big Ban Yan. Or were they under the spell of some mass-hypnosis, digital-age pre-packaged reality, seeing what they expected to see?

Our perceptions are so faulty, I'm thinking as we continue down the goddamn interminable road in the heat. It's hard to tell what's right in front of you, much less learn to distinguish what's real from unreal. My head feels ajar, like I'm allergic, or how I imagine a migraine might be. I'm also limping.

That evening, after a rest back at the hotel, we walk up to a restaurant at the top of the famous Madikeri hill, Raja's Seat. It's too dark for a view. The electricity goes out when we arrive. The cab ride back is through blank blackness.

"Madikeri is so awful," I groan. Surely this place is to blame for my malaise.

"What do you mean?" Antonio asks. "I think it's amazing here."

Suddenly, in some strange alchemy, whatever I see, Antonio sees the opposite.

"Ever since we arrived, I've just wanted to leave," I say.

Odd, Antonio points out, considering I usually find places like this irresistible—quiet, new plants, natural places to investigate. "Perhaps your Madikeri loathing is a reaction to our Mysore interlude?" he suggests.

Possibly. I'd chosen Mysore. As our autorickshaw whizzed into a roundabout on the way to our hotel, a majestic, red-domed palace had blurred past. When we swerved to miss a turmeric-coloured cow lying in our lane, my Canadian Tire water bottle had gone flying out like a high-speed missile, and we'd laughed with pleasure at the chaos. But Mysore, we found, was different from the India we'd experienced in towns and cities of the other southern states of Kerala and Tamil Nadu. Modern, used to foreigners. More familiar.

In Mysore, we stayed in a hotel, versus in ashrams. The restaurant had "Chinese vegetables," to Antonio's relief. He'd been craving plain food. He'd refused to eat any more *sambar*, a popular South Indian lentil-and-vegetable stew, or coconut chutney, and he was getting hungrier, and thinner. When the plate of veggies arrived, it glistened with raw egg whites drizzled over the top, but he dug in without hesitation. We even tried our first Indian red wine, from Grover Vineyards in the nearby Nandi hills, followed by others from the "Krishna Valley," further north, but still in Karnataka state.

I'd been planning some yoga explorations in Mysore, but couldn't track down my friend's teacher, and I found the busy studios unreceptive to people simply passing through. Then I met a type-A Ashtanga yoga student in the street. He was studying with Pattabhi Jois. I asked where else he'd been. "I'm here to study, not here to be a tourist," he sniffed.

I realized that unlike the student, right then I was more interested in sightseeing than in yoga or pilgrimages to spiritual sites. Antonio and I visited a funky cultural centre that showcased arts from rural India, where we bought our only keepsake, a hanging candelabra made of iron that featured monkeys, water buffalo, egrets, and antelope—and sharp edges that punctured our clothes for the rest of the trip.

We headed for Bombay Tiffany's to feast on the "Mysore pak" sweets, made from chickpea flour, sugar, and ghee. Across the hectic street was Mysore's visually stunning market, a vision of life's pleasing abundance: heaped orange and yellow marigolds and fragrant jasmine flowers; tilaka rice powders—bright red, yellow, purple, green, orange, and blue—piled high on platters, and used for anointing the forehead; towers of oranges and onions; burlap bags spilling hot peppers; unfamiliar greens; perfumes and sandalwood and incense. Happy wanderers, we drank in the sights, smells, tastes, textures, sounds.

At times, hundreds of Pallas eagles soared above us. We strolled past cows asleep in the road, or they'd trot alongside us down the streets. In the hardware-store area of town, we watched a worker in flip-flops and shorts climb inside a big metal pot, where he sat down and started to weld—no goggles, sparks flying everywhere. The autorickshaw drivers, as ever, hounded us. When we begged them to leave us alone they'd act hurt, as though we were nasty visitors who would not accept help from kind local people.

Antonio developed what I called "the hand mudra," which mysteriously warded them off: he'd push his open palm toward them gently, and they'd leave. Later, I discover that his symbolic gesture mirrors the Buddhist Abhaya Mudra, perhaps explaining its power. Abhaya translates from Sanskrit as fearlessness.

When I learned the myth of its presiding deity, the goddess Chamundi who slew the male demon Mahishasura, I liked Mysore even more. For the first time in months, I realized, I didn't feel like a second-class citizen. Everywhere we'd been, it was considered forward for a woman to look a man in the eye. As the only woman on a train for hours, I spent a lot of time looking down. At least that way I wasn't encouraging "Eve teasing," a euphemism for sexual harassment. On trains, on packed ferries, men would press up against me. Soon I realized it's forbidden for men and women who don't know one another to touch. So this was risqué, offensive. I began using my elbows to give a swift dig in the ribs to anyone who came too close. The patriarchal miasma, to a greater degree than I'd been aware, had been dampening my spirits.

Yes, I decide, Antonio is right—after Mysore, Madikeri feels like a return to conservatism, to in-your-face India, and my head is rebelling. Earlier in our travels, I'd opened all my doors and windows wide to new ideas and landscapes, courting the unexpected, seeking what was real. But now? I'm exhausted, and the mediated, touristic reality-bubble had been a relief.

The next morning, instead of resting, which would have been intelligent, we head off for a forty-kilometre bus ride to Bylakuppe, near Kushalnagar, the largest Tibetan community outside the Himalayas. The bus zips along, making a stop at a station with washrooms so horrible that Antonio advises me not to enter. The passengers mill around and

I buy a juice. "Thank you for being a Mango lover," the package says. "Thank you for enjoying the King of Fruits with passion. Thank you for making Mango Frooti India's most trusted fruit beverage brand."

We all get back on the bus. Now a newspaper rests on our seat. I flip through it, admire the unfamiliar looping script, and tuck it down the side of the seat. I watch out the window for signs to make sure we don't miss our stop, which should be approaching.

About fifteen minutes on from the bus station, a loud voice says in English, "I want my seat." I see a tall Indian man standing in the aisle, glaring. I wonder whether he's from the north. The southerners we've met tend to be small and mild.

"I want my seat," he repeats.

"But this isn't your seat," I reply, puzzled.

"It is my seat. That's my newspaper."

Antonio and I look at one another. We'd noticed in Kerala that when a bus pulled into the station, people would run toward it, and then throw newspapers in the open windows. This was how they reserved untaken spots.

"Oh," I say, wondering whether it's the same convention here. "Tell me, what difference does it make if you sit here or there?" I ask, pointing to his vacant seat. The man had been sitting directly behind us all this time.

"I want my seat," he repeats.

He has this look of: "No foreigners are going to mess with me." Considering India's history, we'd been surprised never to encounter this attitude, not once.

This man is big and aggressive. I'm really, really fed up with Indian men. I wish I could carbonize him in a blast of fiery flame. "You are being unreasonable," I say.

"I want my seat."

Antonio and I shrug at one another. It's obvious there's been some misunderstanding. It's silly, and hardly worth an international incident. So we move.

There are no other seats together, so I sit one seat behind, where the angry man had been, and Antonio sits across the aisle. This creates great embarrassment for the old man now seated beside me. In south India, many buses are segregated. It's not appropriate for men and women to sit next to one another. The old man flees to the back of the bus. Now Antonio comes and sits beside me. Now we're one seat back from the angry man, who sits, looking triumphant, two seats to himself, in front of us.

That settled, we see the name of our transfer town on a shop sign and leap to our feet. As the bus stops, people push their way on, and the driver has to curse them so they part and let us off. We stand in the heat, dazed.

An autorickshaw pulls over to take us the rest of the way, to the town of displaced Tibetans. En route, the driver scolds me: I'd rested my foot on a footrest that, apparently, isn't to be sullied by feet—or maybe a woman's feet?

I've now left the cold hell of the hotel and the hot hell of Madikeri and entered male incivility hell. I'm annoyed to the roots of my hair. It's as though I'm fighting myself, and everything else. Just then, a maroon-robed monk buzzes past in another autorickshaw. He's a beautiful sight, with his broad brown face and wide smile. I long to arrive at the temple where I can sit and regain some equanimity.

Inside the grounds, the Namdroling Monastery's solemn Golden Temple is full of magnificent paintings and huge, golden Buddhas. Gratitude sweeps me when I see the blue visitor cushions. I sit cross-legged on my precious blue circle of welcome, feeling overwrought. It's a comfort to sit and breathe. After a while, tears pour down my face, and the peculiar frustration that has been building begins to ease. My head feels a little better—as though I'm letting off steam alone in the quiet.

More time passes. An insistent whirring sound breaks the silence. I open my eyes, wipe away tears. A barrage of Indian tourists stands in front of me, smiling and taking my photo. I want to scream.

Instead, I get up and examine the extravagant temple paintings. I'm most drawn to ones that appear to be depictions of hell. The images—in which everyone looks variously tormented, in pain, on fire, frozen, or angry—confirm something I had read. Buddhist hells are divided into hot and cold varieties. And hell beings can be recognized mainly by their acute aggression.

Still thinking about hell states and the implications of my recent hostility—Have I become a hell being? Are they what's afflicting me?—I meet Antonio outside. We walk around the monastery grounds and I have this feeling of displacement. Perhaps being in this community of 16,000 refugees is heightening my melancholy, activating my old feeling of never being in the right place. Is that how we all feel on some level, living our ephemeral lives on earth? All rootless, in transit, on our way to oblivion—or home?

We encounter the Indian family with the whirring cameras again, and stop to chat. They're very sweet, from Kerala, and invite us to visit their home. We take their camera and snap photos of them posing beside landmarks, and bid them a fond goodbye. For lunch, we head down the road to eat at the monastery. A Canadian woman we meet there likes me. She also contradicts every single thing Antonio says. We share a tasty meal of tofu and vegetables, and Antonio cares less about her rudeness.

The bus ride back to Madikeri is uneventful. I feel brighter. We've resolved to leave the next day. We'll go over the mountains back to Kerala and the sea. We're heading to a place that I've chosen, on the fabled spice coast of Malabar. At Madikeri's bus station, we ask about schedules for a bus to Kannur, a town near our inn in Malabar. I want to hire a Jeep taxi, but Antonio says, "It's just over the hill, only 116 kilometres." That's the same distance as the bus ride from Mysore, which took two hours. I agree reluctantly, if we can please take an executive bus—air conditioned, with windows that close, a bus that is direct.

Buses can spell trouble for Antonio and me. They highlight the difference between us as travellers—as people. I like to have some plan and to avoid discomfort. Regular meals, a decent place to sleep. I like to know where the bus is going. Antonio, whose motto is, "If you're not on the road, you're in a rut," is in no hurry, has no agenda. He just wants to get on the path, be open, and travel like the local people do, whatever that entails.

It's true that the unforeseen is what I most love about travelling. Travel, for me, is less about the exploration of places, more about explorations into the nature of being, and consciousness. Discoveries are made uniquely possible by journeys into unknown territory, both geographical and conceptual. But right now, I'm sick, and after months of travels in India, nearing the end of my line. I long for some predictability.

The next morning when Antonio goes to buy the tickets, he is told no buses will leave that day for Kannur. The previous afternoon, we'd asked ten different people, and had been told ten different schedules. The hotel clerk had checked for us too, and said there was a bus at nine thirty. We grab our bags and head for the station, and hope.

Despite the Saturday crowds, my irascibility, and that he's carrying my bag as well as his own yet again, Antonio remains imperturbable. An old man, some sort of official, waves us toward a full bus. It's vagabond, dented, like an ancient school bus. It might be heading our way. We can't be sure. "What to do?" as people here say.

"Better to go somewhere, than to stay here," Antonio reasons. "So let's go and trust it will be okay." I agree, bent on getting out of Madikeri.

We take the last seats, in the back left corner. Across the aisle, a huge tire is wedged across both seats. As the bus rolls forward, local people ask us what sounds like "Canada?" Wondering how they know, we nod, yes. This elicits a torrent of speaking, which puzzles us. Later we learn they were saying "Kannada?"—the name of their language—asking if we spoke it. Despite the mix-up, it's nice to be treated with friendliness instead of aggression. Maybe things are looking up?

After ten more minutes of bumping along, Antonio says, "This bus is going to Thalaserry."

I stare at him in alarm. "Where is Thalaserry?"

He shrugs.

"Is it anywhere near Kannur?"

He shrugs again, unconcerned. He'd tried to find out, but answers had ranged from one hour to six hours away.

For me, it's more stressful to know the name of the destination with no idea where it is. It gives one-pointed focus—Thalaserry, Thalaserry—to my discomfort, worse than my previous no-destination, free-floating anxiety.

What a vile way to spend the day: sick—my throat and my ear are killing me—roasting hot; hungry, as we'd had no time for breakfast; squished in with our luggage between Antonio and a man who changes each station. All this on a bone-rattling road with a driver who honks the horn every five seconds.

I recover a little and dig around in my bag until I find a tourism brochure from a local trekking company. We had been considering a paddy field walk, a plantation walk, and a river bath before we realized that for me, nothing in Madikeri would ever be right. The glossy photos are lovely. I banish an insane thought—we need to start our travels here next time. I consult the brochure, searching for information about Thalaserry. At the top it says in English "road map of Kodagu district." Promising. I squint at faint squiggles on the paper as the bus jolts along. I can't even tell if I'm looking at the state line or the coast. Place names are illegible.

My head whistles and throbs. This is exactly what I'd conjured in my nightmare of the way to Kannur, what I'd tried to avoid. Yet here I am, in the middle of some self-fulfilling prophecy. The bus speeds down the rutted road, swerving around craters while dust pours in windows. I try to breathe through my white shawl. Dusty hell realm.

We hang on tightly to the metal bar on the back of the seat in front of us. Every time we hit a bump, the seat bounces way up, and our hands on the bar are often lower than our asses until the seat crashes back down.

Between speeding, we stop everywhere: bus stops, market towns, whenever someone waves or holds out a bag of chicken or a melon for delivery to friends further down the road. The driver keeps blasting his infernal horn.

No way out. High misery quotient. About three hours in, no idea where we are, I need to pee. The bus stops in a busy market town. I hurry off to find a washroom while Antonio stays with our bags. I walk into the crowd, see a lovely woman in her thirties drinking chai, and head straight for her. She points: a spotless little brick house where a man charges a few rupees to use his spotlessly clean washroom. The chaos always seems worse than it is, I remind myself.

I return to the square, but now it looks different. Many other buses have pulled up. In the swirl of the market, I realize I have no idea where our bus was parked. I walk fast in a panic. Miraculously, I look up and see Antonio.

The bus speeds off again, now nearing the border of the states of Karnataka and Kerala. If the road was bad before, now it's nonexistent.

No one assumes responsibility for the road here. A grey area for paving. We slow to a crawl. I pray, to I don't know whom, "Please, don't let the bus break down in no man's land."

Antonio is getting happier and happier. In hindsight, I see he was trying to cheer me up. Competing realities: pilgrim heart versus grim heart. Not that Antonio's some enlightened sage: oftentimes, our roles are reversed. But what could explain our divergent experiences, our polarized realities, on this particular journey?

He points outside, to the jungle. "Isn't it amazing?" He's probably gesturing at flowering vines, cardamom plantations, bamboo trees, and coffee estates, all of which supposedly thrive here. All I see is the sheer drop down into a canyon below the edge of an escarpment. The bus teeters along. This goes on for an hour. Incredibly, most of the other passengers are asleep.

"Look, an elephant," Antonio says. A man we'd met had told us you could hear meandering pachyderms cracking bamboo trees in the distance. But I'm jaded, thinking it will likely be another Big Ban Yan charade, so I don't even unwrap my head from my shawl.

When Antonio says, "Look how beautiful the trees are," I snap: "I'm trying to give a shit." *Why do I follow him?* I ask myself, as I have so many times in so many situations like this, often involving a bus, on three continents.

Antonio picked Madikeri and got us into this mess. When I'm at my worst, I blame him, even though I know that's absurd. I'm the character in the pith helmet in the jungle from a cartoon I like. The caption reads, "Ok, I admit it, we're lost, but the important thing to remain focused on is whose fault it is." This is a new low in shared bus-hell experiences. For Antonio, it's likely a new low in dealing with my anger, negativity, and neurosis. At this moment, anyway, I do not like being lost.

How can the same trip be so different for two people on the same bus? Despite everything, a small, detached part of me is fascinated. Antonio's eyes are shining: he's genuinely enjoying this. My eyes are barely visible from the dust, and my head pounds in a way I've never experienced. Tension keeps gathering. I feel increasingly trapped and frightened and claustrophobic. It's a disharmonic convergence of ill-will, pain, and self-pity.

I sit with it, and suddenly, it's as though I'm seeing myself from outside my body. Awareness dawns, clear as a voice telling me: *You can either stop breathing and die on the spot now, or get through this*. My breath suspends itself in a moment of utter misery—and then I breathe in.

I've stopped struggling, let go, surrendered, at least a little, to this unpleasant experience. *Maybe all the yoga and meditation is working?* Relax in the presence of tension. Learn patience, self-control, equanimity. Yoga teaches that when we can be unaffected by outer circumstances, it will help us discover our true self.

Mid-epiphany, the bus grinds to a halt. Flat tire. So now we're in this jungle, likely overrun by tigers, wild pigs, cheetahs, and leopards, between two states on a remote unpaved road, on a broken-down bus, heading to who knows where. When this cosmic joke fails to make me laugh, I know I'm truly sick and exhausted.

It's time to go home, I think. Two small Indian men haul the spare tire out of the back seat beside us with amazing efficiency. *End of the line.* Antonio follows them, trying to help. They give him an odd look, but let him pick up the wheel. He burns his hand on the hot metal rim, and then leaves them to it. He says later that's when he realized this was their job; he'd interfered. How easy it is to upset the social order, to fall afoul of the Hindu caste system, which officially no longer exists in India. And this is what happens when you do, Antonio jokes—you get burned.

Within an hour we're underway again. This pit stop, it seems, is a routine event. As usual, what seemed out of control from my perspective is revealed to be absolutely fine.

We reach Thalaserry in six hours, versus the two we'd estimated. I insist on stopping for a meal, so we have our usual disagreement—now that we're close, Antonio's in a hurry to get to our destination. Over vegetarian thali we learn that miraculously, or Antonio would say naturally, Kannur is just twenty kilometres north of Thalaserry. The hotel is part-way to Kannur, so we've landed a very short distance away.

Back in the confusion of the bus station, autorickshaw drivers study our paper with the name of the place we're going. None of them know it. Antonio asks me to watch our bags while he finds someone who does. After ten minutes he rounds the corner and makes his way through the crowd with a big smile on his face—and a one-legged man with a long white beard in a white sarong hopping after him on crutches.

I groan inwardly, anxiety rebounding. *We are so fucked.* Of all the unlikely looking helpers, this man tops them all. He asks us for a rupee and makes a phone call. Then he shakes our paper with the address on it at the drivers, chooses one man, and tells him something firmly. The one-legged man helps us climb in, gives us our rupee back, waves curtly, and hops off.

Relief is short-lived: it's soon apparent that the driver doesn't know the way. All of us, strangers in strange lands, travelling without a map. The driver stops and asks people along the road. They wave their arms around, and we head down a new road.

Another autorickshaw has been honking at us, racing ahead, then falling behind. Drivers often do this for fun, so I'd taken little notice. Oddly, though, our driver has been ignoring the other driver. I motion to say, "Do you know them?" and he shakes his head, the side-to-side Indian head wobble that can mean many things. The other driver overtakes us again, and a man yells in English, "We met you in Kushalnagar!" It's the family from the Tibetan monastery, smiling and waving madly.

Lost in the middle of nowhere, and friends have found us. Finally, something makes me smile. We wave back at them, and soon speed around a bend, where they don't follow. Now we're going down a narrow road cut into the earth, like a half-tunnel. Our driver is on his cell phone, talking to our host, whose phone number we'd given him. We aren't lost at all.

We see a small man in a jean shirt and sarong sitting at a little table having a drink with a friend. He waves, and hops on his motorbike to escort us to Costa Malabari. The quiet house stands in a coconut palm grove, set on a cliff above a gorgeous beach. Delivered.

The driver charges so little that we make him accept more. Antonio insists I go for a swim. The sea is warm, the waves playful, the view restful: red rocks, green palms and trees, and raptors circling high above. Some boys emerge from the bushes and hand me "Kerala food, lilica fruit," which they say sour pickles are made from.

After my swim, I feel healed: even my sore ear is better. I'm meant to be by water. From here, in a few days, we will make our way down the coast by train, back to Cochin for a yoga retreat. Then we'll fly to Dubai, London, and Toronto. I'm feeling ready to go home. But right now, this place is the perfect balm for a tired and wired spirit.

After a sleep, I go outside, find a chair overlooking the beach. My mind's "bad space" trickles away into the wave sounds. I sip a mango lassi and watch two fishermen in a sinking boat. I wonder if they're having the same experience.

How is it possible that Antonio took pleasure in the Thalaserry bus, despite heat, dust, uncertainty, and my poisonous negativity?

I'm captivated by the idea of the bus, of being in transit. It seems to allow unique glimpses of the mind's landscape as it moves through changing geographies. Antonio had been open and accepting of experience. He passed through discomfort, but didn't try to escape. Since, arguably, all creatures will experience uneasiness and anxiety because comfort isn't sustainable, his approach seems wise. He'd stayed in the present moment, and found much that was pleasing.

For my part, I'd taken it all personally, blaming Madikeri, tourism websites, Antonio, illness, patriarchy, hell-beings, mix-ups, misunderstanding, and chaos, among other things, for my misery. The Buddhists, I decide, are right: hell is a state of mind, not a place. Reality is what we *perceive*, versus what *is*.

Refreshed by a second mango lassi, I get out my journal. "Travellers, who literally don't know what's around the next corner, must surrender to the unknown, life's ever-changing flow, and find their own meaning," I write with a flourish. The trip had been awful, but illuminating. And while I want to loathe the experience properly, it just feels good to have survived.

That evening, lulled by wave sounds, we sit at a communal table under the coconut palms and swap travellers' tales. The other guests talk about elephants in the nearby Wayanad wildlife sanctuary and discuss the fascinations of *theyyam*, a local performance ritual that pre-dates Hinduism. When Antonio tells them about our good day, "moving, going somewhere, seeing the green, and taking a really wild ride in the mountains," I smile, and nod in agreement.

The Retreat

WE CLIMB INTO THE WHITE HINDUSTAN AMBASSADOR AND luxuriate on the sofa-like back seat. Instead of his usual pink sweatpants, Ani is wearing a saffron *lungi*—a South Indian sarong.

After our long trip to Cochin, Antonio and I are grateful to see our friend. Ani is a little brother of a man: small, sweet, with a quick laugh. Dear to everyone. He's also one of the first yoga teachers I studied with in Toronto. Ani's charm, gentle wisdom, and devotion to the path of yoga have kept me in his orbit.

We speed away from the airport on the "wrong" side of the road in a melee of other Ambassadors, black-and-yellow autorickshaws, and motorbikes that swerve around goats and cows. A grape-purple bus thunders by, festooned with marigold garlands and stickers of Jesus and Ganesha, the elephant-god. Destroyer of obstacles.

We're a long way from Ani's yoga studio in Toronto and our home in Kingston—15,000 kilometres away. Yet I feel certain that this three-week "yoga intensive" in Ani's home village, where his family lives, will deepen my understanding of stillness and help me to become a better yoga teacher.

After driving through a busy town—the closest one to his village, Ani says—we enter the green countryside, where we wind through palm groves and over small canals. Water buffalo, ropes looped through their noses, watch us pass. Bumping onto a red-earth track that cuts through emerald tapioca fields, we reach the village and pull up at Ani's yoga school—at first glance, a graceful, two-storey house ringed by tall coconut palms.

We hoist our bags out of the trunk and onto the wide verandah. Garbage is piled high. Inside, everything looks dirty. I wasn't expecting this, I think groggily. Ani shows us to a room with a mattress on the floor. He hands us bed sheets and two bottles of water. "You can rest here for now," he says.

That's when I notice the noise. Unbeknownst to him, Ani explains, a brickyard has opened up next door. A sound like they're sawing cement, and a radio is blasting vertigo-inducing music I've only ever heard in Bollywood movies.

The room spins now that we have finally stopped our perpetual motion. I dig out the construction earplugs, hand a set to Antonio. "Let's try to sleep. Things will seem better when we wake up," I say.

I think back to our flight from Dubai to Cochin, a bright moon floating in the dark blue sky. An auspicious sign; I had read that the moon rises during meditation when one attains a deeper level of calm.

Right now, earplugs firmly intact, I can still hear sawing. *What kind of sign is this?* I wonder, plummeting towards sleep.

When we awaken a few hours later, we see white walls stained with monsoon rot, dust layering every surface. Mouse shit is abundant. Ani says he tried to pay someone from the village to clean up, but no one would. The place had been closed for nine years.

The retreat starts in four days.

That evening, Ani leaves to stay with his parents. Antonio and I are alone in the silent ashram. The long trip and searing heat leave us wanting to drink and drink, but we have little fresh water, and there's none here. Should we go out to buy water? And where exactly would we go?

A droning engine approaches around nine o'clock. An autorickshaw lurches up out of the night, and two laughing women descend with bag upon bag of purchases. I watch them from the upstairs balcony with relief. Merry people! I rush down to meet them.

"Come and see what we bought," Maya calls as Dorothea waves us back upstairs. Their room has a pretty paper star hanging on the door. The bed is decorated with a pink mosquito net. I watch as they pull out cotton housedresses—"You have to get some when we go to town"—and display new cotton bras with freaky missile breasts. Antonio and I gratefully accept a bottle of water. Dorothea encourages us to move upstairs and away from the brickyard. Upstairs, she says, "the noise sucks less."

Our new room has a large ceiling fan, a cement shelf built into the wall, a window with iron bars, and a heavy wooden bed frame. This room's been cleaned, colourful straw mats adorn the black polished cement, and there's a bathroom. Perfect, we agree, as we drape our mosquito net over the bed.

Next morning, we help Maya and Dorothea to clean up, while Ani visits relatives. The three of them had been travelling in France and Holland, and had just recently arrived themselves. I jump as hand-sized black spiders scuttle out from behind whatever object we move. "That's nothing," Maya says. "We found the mattresses all piled up in one room. When we pulled one down, dozens of mice came leaping out." Antonio and I groan. We drag our bed outside, douse it with DEET, and leave it baking in the sun.

One afternoon, we take a break and ride the bus to town, where local people stare and smile. We are celebrities, of sorts. An old lady with no teeth comes up to Kevin, Maya's twenty-two-year-old son. She's laughing, motioning to his *lungi*. It's on backwards.

Signs advertise "unlimited free STDs." This, Maya explains, is where you go to use the telephone—standard trunk dialing. We learn how to cross the street: walk into traffic quickly and pray that vehicles swerve around you.

The sun's incessant beating, combined with car fumes, gives new meaning to the word "exhaustion." Sitting on a curb to drink a reviving chai, I try not to think about unpasteurized milk or hepatitis. The other customers use this technique for drinking so their lips never touch the cup—they pour the chai into their open mouths, straight from above. When I try this, the liquid curdles down my front.

Kevin laughs at me. That's fine. What makes me cringe is his calling out to passersby, "Hashish?"—thus confirming what many Indians think about depraved Westerners. In a futile attempt to cool off, I buy some talcum powder. "A mist of hypnotic charm," the label says. "Mind-blowing & alluring aroma. An unforgettable experience enriched your feelings."

Slowly, other yoga students begin to arrive until we are twelve in all. Canadians. The group includes a carpenter, two university professors, a public health nurse, a student activist, a graphic designer, and a fitness instructor. Dorothea is a film editor, and Maya owns the gas station where Kevin works. All but one person have studied with Ani in the past. Many of us are also yoga teachers.

The night before the retreat begins, spirits are high. We chat on the balcony upstairs, looking out at the green mountain. Ani notices that we've been taking turns reading a book we'd found while cleaning up. It's by Swami Sivananda—the guru of his guru, Swami Vishnu-Devananda.

"Don't look at what it says about women," Ani makes a face.

"Too late, we've read it," I say. "So sexist."

"Even gurus mess up," he replies with a shrug.

I'm relieved when the retreat gets underway. At first, we all focus on yoga and fall into the ashram rhythm of full, structured days, beginning at five thirty. The faraway sound of drums and temple song carries, otherworldly, on the wind. We gather for *satsang*—meditation, chanting, and a lecture—from six to seven thirty, and then for yoga class from eight to ten. Our yoga room is in an unfinished building that will eventually serve as the kitchen for Ani's brother's catering business. I don't envy those who didn't bring their own yoga mats as they perform headstands on thin rush mats atop the lumpy concrete floor.

After class, we walk up to Ani's mother's house for breakfast. Then it's a little time to wash clothes, nap, or read—despite the brickyard racket—until the two o'clock lecture. Then yoga again, from four to six, followed by dinner at six thirty at "Mum's" and satsang from eight o'clock until nearly ten thirty.

All day, one moment flows effortlessly into the next.

In the "never hurry, never stop" tempo of our days, Antonio and I have the most contact with the other upstairs dwellers, especially Maya and Dorothea. They have a shelf stocked with cookies from Holland, chocolates from Paris, and Greens Plus; they also have every medical remedy known to man. The women share generously.

Maya even bought an electric burner so we could make coffee—and boil drinking water. She creates a sense of community, and Antonio and I are grateful. At dawn, we sit on the upstairs balcony with our cups of instant coffee, gazing wordlessly out at the mountain.

Dorothea, who is constantly saying lewd things and swearing in Dutch, keeps me laughing. She bellows lines from *Young Frankenstein*, a film we both love. "Remember when Madeline Kahn gets it on with the monster? 'At last I've found you.'" She tells disgusting stories about parasites and chilling tales of being sexually harassed in Varanasi, where she spent three months learning to play the sitar.

The downstairs dwellers are another story. Two laid-back profs in their fifties, a new student who left a course at another ashram to join ours, two thirty-something women. Ani. Some have rooms. Others have pitched tents beside the ashram.

During our yoga classes with Ani, I'm impressed once more by his skill in teaching *asanas*, the yoga postures, and by the way he connects with students. I'm inspired to watch the advanced yogis twisting into poses I've never seen anyone perform, and to try new ones myself. Being a student again, taking a break from yoga teaching and my other work, I feel free.

The village's eternal rhythms also induce peace. Tall coconut palms sway, fronds clacking in the wind. Kingfishers flash electric blue in the treetops. Out back, a woman in a sari leads three goats on strings. Other women in bright turbans work the tapioca fields. White egrets freeload on the backs of grazing water buffalo. Time slows. Once in a while, things feel so harmonious that I think I could even live in a crazy little community like this one.

Then, the irritations. People struggle with wicked colds, insomnia, and constipation. The South Indian diet is unfamiliar. Although it's vegetarian, it's high on rice and low on fresh vegetables. There is little drinking water. There is forty-plus-degree heat. One day, Ani announces he will collect money to buy water. This does not go over well. Eventually, he purchases an electric burner like Maya's, so the people downstairs can boil water too.

The day we do *kriyas*, cleansing practices, there's little water, as usual. For this exercise, we are going to drink eight cups of salt water each, and then throw up. The last time I had done this, years before, I'd felt weak and dehydrated. I pass on the practice.

I tell Antonio about my previous ashram experiences. Normally, day-to-day concerns about living space and meals are well organized so that students can focus on learning. Why is Ani so unprepared? There's litter everywhere. Out front is a canal that's full of eels. People and water buffaloes bathe in that canal—our water source, we realize. We've been taking showers in that water, boiling it to drink. The public health nurse develops a tic under her eye and insists we all accept bottles of hand sanitizer.

Oh, and explosions. Over the sawing of the bricks, we hear repeated explosions. Maya says they come from where the mountain used to be, out back. The mountain is no longer visible; it's been mined away completely. Ani is also disappearing—into one young woman's tent. They giggle together, like kids. Someone asks me if they are lovers. I dismiss this as a silly notion. In the mornings, Ani is often late to lead the six o'clock silent meditation.

When not feeling at one with everything, I also notice how distracted I am getting. My mind wanders ceaselessly during meditation. That floating moon I'd seen on the flight, my bright omen of deepening calm? It's definitely not rising. Instead, I'm caught in wave after wave of resentment toward Ani. I'm troubled by the upstairs/downstairs rift, with the malcontents upstairs, the keeners down.

Maya and Dorothea quit smoking. They start again. They try to hide it from Maya's son, Kevin. Ani is smoking too. One day, he gives a rambling lecture about the difference between yoga and Vedanta—which, translated, means "the end of knowledge."

I'd been looking forward to this, one of the main topics to be covered. The ancient sage Adi Sankara, an adept of the Kevala Advaita Vedanta path—the pure, non-dualistic school of Vedanta—was originally from South India; he had summarized the essence of Vedantic teachings in three statements: *God only is real. The world is unreal. The individual is none other than God.*

But as Ani talks, clarity does not come. I wonder, is it just me? Or do all his lectures seem unfocused? I'm more interested in Kevin's efforts to find a loophole in the laws of karma. He's started speaking with an Indian accent that makes him sound like Peter Sellers in *The Party*. Maybe Kevin has the right idea. During lectures he stretches out on the ground, appears to be sleeping. Once in a while, Ani asks, "Right Kevin?"

"Right," Kevin says.

The questions I thought I'd be engaging on retreat have been replaced by "What's biting me?" "Where can I get some water?" "What the hell is going on?"

Early the first week, "Swamiji" arrives. Ani explains that they had studied together for a decade in the ashram when they were in their twenties, and that Swamiji will teach a few classes. His car, a black Ford with blacked-out windows, looks like a yogi-pimpmobile. It features a fancy "Om" symbol in orange on the windshield. The car seats, Kevin tells me, are covered in fake fur.

Swamiji's classes run as follows: "Sit down. Sit straight," he orders. He instructs us to question him in order to draw out his "deep knowledge," but when someone does ask, he barks, "I already told you." He rambles nonsensically in poor English or replies with a kingly air, "You can't possibly understand." At one point he says, "Ask Ani about yoga, and ask me about spiritual matters." He talks about using yoga to gain powers to fight enemies, to walk on water. What about seeking truth, or perhaps becoming a more peaceful, sane person?

One night, he tells us that the best way to sit in meditation is on the skin of a deer or a tiger—but only one that died of natural causes.

"Have you experienced this?" Maya asks with a devilish grin.

"Yes, I had a tiger skin."

"The animal died of natural causes?"

"Yes, the tiger was electrocuted when it touched an electric fence."

We all exchange looks, laugh out loud, when Maya says under her breath, "So how exactly is electrocution 'natural causes?'"

"I sat on the skin a few times and it was powerful. I gave it away though," he adds. "I didn't want animal rights people saying I was killing tigers or something."

We tell Ani that we don't want any more classes with "Ji"—the diminutive means "little"—but Ani insists that he wants us to see "how yoga is taught in India." Ji has been sleeping in his car, trying shamelessly to snare some Western students of his own—us.

He keeps talking about his nearby yoga centre in a neighbouring state. I tell Kevin that Ji has a centre in the "state of Karnataka." He thinks it's like a state of *samadhi*, or nirvana.

Yoga teachers often emphasize how the physical practice of yoga— hatha yoga—is not as important as its wider philosophical and spiritual foundations. "It's level one, please go beyond and bring yoga into your life," Ani says.

Here, for me, at least, the poses are by far the most fruitful part of the day.

Walking along the canal after class one morning, a yoga insight arises out of the stillness. My steps feel heavy. I think of Ani, and the words form: *This is your disappointment to bear. Let this experience be what it is,* I think. *Accept it.*

For a little while, it's a relief to let go.

The upstairs/downstairs split continues to deepen: skeptics on the top floor, acolytes on the bottom. Two young women from downstairs chant nonstop, "Vande gurudev, jaya jaya gurudev." We mimic flinging things at them from the balcony.

The skeptics are giving up on the retreat. Antonio reads the Krishnamurti books he'd brought from home, meditates on the roof, and joins us only for yoga class and meals. Kevin practices "naked yoga"—likely a few poses and a nap—up on the roof, or hangs out with his friends. Young men from the village sit with him on the bridge in the evenings. I love Kevin's reports of these conversations. "They say we are like animals with clothes," he tells me one night, referring to Western sexual practices. His friends will have arranged marriages, most likely when they're in their twenties.

I skip classes too. In the village, the tailors play chess outside, and I have chai or buy beets, beans, and lentil and jaggery balls for dinner so we won't have to eat with the group. I take an autorickshaw into town to buy water. I do anything to avoid Ji's *Bhagavad Gita* classes. He takes this spiritual gem, this masterpiece of Sanskrit poetry and world literature, and tortures each *sutra*. There are 700 verses.

Ani's lectures are growing worse. Someone—a devotee from downstairs—comments on how his discourses are spirals, how he adds a new piece of information each time. I once thought that, too, I realize. In addition to lectures, Ani has now asked Ji to lead evening meditation. Ani complains that he doesn't have enough time to teach and to see his relatives, the retreat is *a lot of work*. The course is fifteen days long, minus three days off. Twelve days of teaching.

Seven days into the retreat Ji starts leading evening *satsang*. I give him a chance, but after the fourth time, I stay in my room. One night, he comes upstairs to round us up, calling, "Students, come."

On day eight, Ani announces that Ji will also take over afternoon yoga *asana* class. This means we'll be with Ji from two thirty onward, through the evening. And where will Ani be? People complain, yet Ani gives Ji more and more to do. Ani persists, says Ji is an Ayurvedic expert who knows all about plants, and we should take advantage of his knowledge. Soon he is giving treatments, going in and out of rooms and tents.

Carolyn, a beautiful blond fitness instructor, has a skin condition on her scalp. She gets an hour-long treatment that involves a head massage. It also involves taking off her top. I hear Dorothea, who has a similar problem but is less conventionally pretty, say that her treatment lasted all of five minutes, scalp only.

Still, some sensible people from downstairs, men and women, have been having treatments, and I too have a skin condition—for which, I hear, *tulsi* leaves are excellent, so when Ji asks, I agree to a treatment. I lie naked on my sarong on the floor as he plasters green paste all over me. He tells me I can wash it off in half an hour. I feel uncomfortable, but I tell myself that he's okay—he's Ani's friend. They studied together for ten years, didn't they?

One morning during his lecture, Ani tells us that people either love or hate India. I'm not sure where I fit just yet. I vacillate. Ani says to try to drop our expectations, learn to relax.

"India will give you nothing if you come to see old buildings. You need to relax yourself when frustration arises, and it's the best thing for you in those moments."

He says if you learn to relax here it's a gift, as India can be crazy and maddening. So far, what I'm finding crazy and maddening is Ani.

Our day off arrives. We are grateful, and go to visit a local waterfall, returning that evening to good news. Ji, Ani says, has gone because of our feedback. "I understand that you came to India to study with me," Ani says.

In my journal I write, "I hope this improves the focus and depth of the retreat."

The next morning's scuttlebutt is that Ji's departure is due to his behaviour with two female students during "ayurvedic" treatments. In one case, he had dropped his *lungi* during a massage and started talking about tantric sex. Oh, and there was something about a camera hidden under a cloth. And drugged tea.

I feel sick—as does everyone else, especially those of us who had skin treatments with Ji. I tell Ani that I'm angry, trusted this man because he was his friend. Why did Ani ignore us for over a week when we said we didn't want Ji here?

"Do you think I would invite someone here to exploit my family on purpose?" he retorts. He complains that we should have told him if something was wrong because he has lots on his mind, adds that Ji is gone and never coming back, all in a "so drop it" tone of voice.

Ani becomes more organized and focused. He does not apologize, but says, "the worst has happened."

"Is there anything else that needs to be said?" he asks.

No one speaks: a few of us have conversed with him already. And it's odd—the woman who says she was molested, who says that Ji had tried to film and drug her, has shrugged it off, saying, "It's his karma." Another woman Ji touched sexually during a massage says she "handled it."

One night, near the end of our final week, I hear a rickshaw engine's approaching buzz, and wild laughter. Antonio and I watch from the upstairs balcony as three yoga students tumble out of the back seat, drunk.

They try coming upstairs quietly, but when they see us, they crack up. "We had seventeen beers," Maya shouts, awakening everyone in the house.

I go to bed, my head spinning. In the past, Ani taught me valuable, even life-changing lessons. In India, I'd hoped to move to the next level of yoga knowledge, which he certainly possesses.

How then did I end up in a yoga cliché, replete with fake gurus bent on power and sex, tiger skins, and befuddled seekers—including me?

Next morning. Six o'clock meditation. Afterwards, Ani says, "This is not a holiday camp but a serious retreat centre." His voice is stern. The miscreants are still asleep upstairs. After all that's happened, his words sound preposterous.

Today, mercifully, is the last day of classes. Tomorrow's have been cancelled because we've been invited to a Hindu wedding and Amma, the famous "Hugging Saint" of Kerala, will be giving blessings nearby. Antonio and I will then leave for Cochin, and soon, head back home.

In the afternoon, we write a test for our yoga intensive certificates. It's a charade, but I'm in this to the end. At least it's the kind of learning I can relate to. I decide to complete the test with the serious intent that I brought to the retreat.

That night, we gather on the roof of the ashram, in a circle. The sky is dark, black, the stars in unfamiliar southern constellations. There's a big full moon. We are all strangely quiet, Ani comments.

I stare at the tall coconut palm silhouettes swaying in the breeze. Ani continues to talk about how he thinks it was a good retreat. We all sit silent. A huge lump stops up my throat.

I'm sad about my friend and teacher. And about my lost hope of learning, transformation. All journeys hold the potential for a touch, a look, a realization that will change you forever. When we came to study in India, yoga's birthplace, this is what I both feared and hoped for.

I look at that moon, and learn what there is to learn: that no matter what I expect, life will be what it is. Which in this case, I decide, means the same old shit with an Indian flavour.

In the past, Ani's teachings had been exactly what I'd needed, and for that, I remain grateful. But now? I might get to a place of understanding, grasp the secret curriculum, what I'm learning but don't realize I'm learning. But at this moment, I am angry and disappointed.

The retreat officially over, we all lie back in the darkness and gaze at the sky. I think about another yoga teacher of mine, someone back home. Once she had advised: "Trust the path. Trust yourself. Trust the teacher." Then she'd laughed. "No, forget about that last one."

I ponder this a while. My mind turns to Wallace Stevens. Was he the poet who said that the last illusion is disillusion? The moon glimmers, golden in the dark.

PHOTO: Marco Reiter

Kirsteen MacLeod is a writer and yoga teacher who lives in Kingston, Ontario. *The Animal Game* is her debut collection of short fiction. Kirsteen was born in Glasgow, Scotland, lived in Toronto and Brazil, and has worked as a magazine writer and editor, and communicator, for 30 years.

ACKNOWLEDGEMENTS

✸ *The Animal Game* is dedicated to Marco ✸ I'd particularly like to thank Katharine MacLeod, my beloved and supportive sister ★ Helen Humphreys, necessary angel and animating spirit of the 10,000 steps ★ Melanie McCallum, darling friend and DB ★ Bugsy Malone ★ Smokey T-Bone T and Mr. Pinks ★ Janet Crocker, cherished friend and kazillion-time reader of this book ★ Susan Scott, for brilliant editing and great generosity of spirit ★ Gratitude always to Maira, Karin, Ingrit, Aline, Silvana, Janete, Luis, Dona Lurdes, Senhor Osvaldo, *e os queridos Brasileiros—abraços em todos* ★ Dear and adventurous mother Katharine MacLeod ★ Inimitable father Charles MacLeod and his "faraway places with strange-sounding names" ★ The Villanelles—Sarah Tsiang, Wayne Westfall, Heather Browne, Ashley-Elizabeth Best, Jane Kerrison, Susan Olding and Sadiqa de Meijer ★ Writer-pilgrims Anita Jansman and Sarah Withrow ★ The editors of *The New Quarterly*—Susan, Pamela, Kim, and Barbara—who published my work, including many of these stories ★ *The Malahat Review* for publishing the title story ★ The Ontario Arts Council, for financial support while writing this book ★ The CBC Literary Awards, *Malahat*'s Open Season contest, and the Writers' Union contest, for choosing stories in this collection as finalists ★ Jim Nason, Heather Wood and Deanna Janovski of Tightrope Books, for warmth, great enthusiasm and expert bookwrangling ★ Carolyn Smart, professor and inspiration ★ Diane Schoemperlen, for literary largesse ★ The Queen's U Writers in Residence—Helen Humphreys, Diane Schoemperlen, Tim Wynne-Jones, Stuart Ross, Steven Heighton ★ The Gallery Writers—Noreen Macklin, Helen Coo, Judy Wearing, Heather Browne, Sandy Alexander, Margaret Coughlin ★ Cary Silverstein, Jessie Silverstein, Stylistics, Ghandiman International Enterprises, Sheila McCallum, Marilou McCallum, Mango Frooti, Johnny Lucas, Brenda, Ela and Katrina, Ed and Leslie, the Weatherheadians, Eric Tenn, Vishnu, my yoga community, especially students, who teach me more than I teach them, the Janatians, Tiffany Bambrick, RK Narayan, Cervantes, The Beer Drinking Ladies, WG Sebald, Portsmouth Tavern, The Sleepless Goat, Enid Blyton, Clarice Lispector, Coffeeco, the noble grapes of Spain, Jennifer Payne, movement maestra and averter of "felden-crises,"the Banff Centre, Memorial Centre Farmer's Market, Cataraqui Conservation Area, the denizens of Kingscourt, especially Marilyn and Matthew, Alan Morantz, for kindness and threats of profanity, Maureen Jennings and the expressive writers, Don Obe, The Imperial Public Library, HB Beal and John Krisak, Charles Ritchie, and Martin Woollings, Hafiz, Jim Harrison, Jack Gilbert, Elizabeth Bishop, for questions of travel. ★ You. ★ Your blessed self.

IMAGINATION ON THE HIGHWIRE

Tightrope Books
#207-2 College Street,
Toronto Ontario, Canada M5G 1K3
tightropebooks.com
bookinfo@tightropebooks.com